3/7

D0500447

BASEBALL GENIUS

TIM GREEN · DEREK JETER

JETER CHILDREN'S

ALADDIN
New York   London   Toronto   Sydney   New Delhi

ALADDIN
An imprint of Simon & Schuster Children's Publishing Division
1230 Avenue of the Americas, New York, New York 10020
First Aladdin hardcover edition March 2017
Text copyright © 2017 by Tim Green
Jacket illustration copyright © 2017 by Tim Jessell
All rights reserved, including the right of reproduction
in whole or in part in any form.
ALADDIN and related logo are registered trademarks of Simon & Schuster, Inc.
For information about special discounts for bulk purchases,
please contact Simon & Schuster Special Sales at 1-866-506-1949
or business@simonandschuster.com.
The Simon & Schuster Speakers Bureau can bring authors to your live event.
For more information or to book an event contact the Simon & Schuster Speakers
Bureau at 1-866-248-3049 or visit our website at www.simonspeakers.com.
Jacket designed by Jessica Handelman
Interior designed by Mike Rosamilia
The text of this book was set in Centennial LT Std.
Manufactured in the United States of America 0217 FFG
2 4 6 8 10 9 7 5 3 1
This book has been cataloged with the Library of Congress.
ISBN 978-1-4814-6864-0 (hc)
ISBN 978-1-4814-6866-4 (eBook)

For my wife, Illyssa,
and our five amazing children!
—T. G.

To Jalen, who makes every day an adventure
—D. J.

1

JALEN PEERED THROUGH THE WINDOWS OF THE Silver Liner Diner to make sure his father was still busy. A man in a black knit cap sat at the counter with a newspaper, a cup of coffee, and a piece of pie. In one booth a young, awkward-looking couple in fancy clothes scowled at each other, arguing in silence behind the glass. Jalen watched his father deliver two plates of his special stuffed calamari to the couple. While the Silver Liner was a diner, it was also much more: a place for authentic Italian food. While the two didn't seem to go together, Jalen's father somehow seemed to scratch out a living.

When a car drove up with new customers, Jalen knew he had time to sneak off into the spring night. He snugged the empty backpack on his shoulders as he crossed the railroad tracks. Wind picked at his curly hair, and he paused at the wailing sound of a distant train.

Beside the station stood a fast-food place, the lights on its big yellow-and-blue-and-purple sign extinguished for the night, since it closed after the last train arrived from New York. Jalen's dad usually let his help go after dinnertime but squeezed a few extra dollars from the Silver Liner by staying open late, even after midnight, if he had any customers.

Main Street was empty, but Jalen decided to take a detour and avoid the streetlamps. He jogged fifteen minutes to the other side of town, all uphill, to Rockton's oldest and biggest estate. It had been built in 1782 by the great-great-grandfather (step-great-great-grandfather, she'd always point out) of one of his best friends, Cat Hewlett. Its heavy iron gates stood open, but he stopped to catch his breath. Fastened to one of the great stone columns by a thick chain was a bronze plaque letting visitors know they were about to enter Mount Tipton. Jalen wondered what name his home would go by if anyone cared to call it anything. Probably Broken Box or maybe Shabby Shack.

He darted through the gates and into the shadows, avoiding the long, sweeping driveway and the lights buried in the grass alongside it. His friends were waiting for him at the corner of the stables. The rich smell of horse manure swirled deep in Jalen's nose. Daniel Bellone didn't even smell it anymore. He and his family lived above the horses, along with two other families who helped maintain Mount Tipton in all its original glory, trimming the gardens and grass, painting the buildings, scrubbing floors, and polishing the brass and silver when needed.

Cat lived in the big house—as Daniel called it—but with her messy brown hair, scrubby jeans, and the sweatshirt she wore, she looked like she was the one who lived above the stables.

"Ready?" she asked, snapping her gum and cutting the barn smell with a whiff of peppermint. She bumped fists with Jalen. Even Cat's raspy voice and the smudge on her face couldn't hide how pretty she was.

"As I'll ever be." Jalen bumped Daniel's fist, then turned to look down the hill, over the treetops, at the big brick house a quarter mile beyond Mount Tipton's stone wall. The huge mansion sat on a hilltop of its own, bathed in soft yellow light.

Jalen and Cat trudged off down the grassy slope, following Daniel, who knew the way through the tangle of riding trails better than anyone. They skirted the trout pond on a wide, grassy trail before plunging into the woods. The trees above swished in the wind. The beam of the flashlight on Cat's phone flicked this way and that so that shadows of the thick tree trunks danced and jumped. When they reached the high stone wall marking Tipton's boundary, Daniel pulled up.

"You sure about this?" Cat asked Jalen, directing the light at their feet so that its glow lit the three friends' faces.

Jalen was surprised. "Why are you saying this now? We all agreed. It's not like I've got a barrelful of choices."

"I could . . ." Cat's voice drifted off on the wind. She looked toward the estate, but they all knew that her stepfather gave her nothing.

"Maybe . . ." Daniel looked slightly embarrassed. His fee for the travel baseball team had been paid. His spot on the Rockets was secured.

Without words, Jalen tried to tell Daniel that it was okay. Daniel's parents were two of the hardest-working people Jalen had ever seen. It wasn't his fault that Jalen couldn't afford the travel team fees, and Daniel could.

"Just . . . be careful of the dogs." Daniel peered out from beneath a shock of hair as dark as the night and shook his head before uttering his version of a curse. "Hot sauce."

"I know." Jalen patted his pants pocket and the pork chop bones wrapped in plastic tucked inside. He bit his lip and started to climb the rock wall, inserting the toes of his sneakers into the cracks. When he reached the top of the ten-foot wall, he straddled the flat fieldstones and looked down at his friends below.

"Maybe we should go with you?" Daniel's face was hidden in the gloom, and his whisper barely rose above the trees.

"Thanks," Jalen said. "But no. If it goes bad, I could be . . . I don't know. Arrested?"

"I don't think—" Cat began, before a long pause during which her face grew grim. "Maybe."

"So, no sense in taking you guys down too," Jalen said. "Thanks for coming this far."

"We'll wait right here," Daniel said. "We won't leave."

Cat began to climb the wall.

"No, Cat," Jalen said. "I told you."

She reached the top and sat with her legs hanging down on the Tipton side as she held up her phone. "I'll keep it here, in case you get lost. It'll be a beacon."

Jalen gave her leg a pat. "If it's not me for any reason, jump and run."

"It'll be you." Cat's blue eyes glittered, even in the dim light. "You can do this. It'll work, and you'll be on that travel team going up and down the East Coast, knocking in runs and turning twos."

"Thanks." Jalen let himself down a few feet before simply springing away from the wall and dropping to the ground. He didn't look back because he didn't want to chicken out. He plunged into the darkness of the trees, waiting for his eyes to adjust, stumbling through the open woods, his eyes fixed on the lights of the huge brick mansion owned by a New York Yankees star.

Jalen's stomach felt empty and cold and fragile, like a fist in wintertime without a glove. It wasn't just the darkness. It wasn't just being completely alone. It wasn't just the danger.

It was that—despite all the rules Jalen had bent in his life—he'd never taken anything that didn't belong to him.

Never stolen so much as a candy bar.

That was about to change.

2

THE WOODED SLOPE ENDED AT A NARROW CREEK,
easy to hop. The bank on the other side opened onto a
wide grass skirt surrounding the front and sides of the
house on its own hill. The yellow lights in the bushes
around the building lit it from the ground up so that
as he got closer, Jalen could see the diamond-shaped
pieces of glass in windows crosshatched with white trim.
Broad green shutters. Flower boxes filled with color. A
large stone fountain babbled from the circular driveway. Bronze angels struggled skyward for a trumpet
that splashed them all before finding the fountain's wide
pool. Beyond the fountain, a sleek black Lamborghini
rested before the wide steps leading to the front doors.

Jalen kept to the tree line, circling the mansion toward the back. A terrace supported by brick columns looked down over a pool area fenced in wrought iron, but Jalen's target lay beyond that, in a grassy dip hollowed out of the trees, where black netting drooped from tall posts like the forgotten web of a monster-movie spider.

Jalen's heart thumped the underside of his ribs, knocking to get out. There were no floodlights here, only the glow from the pool and the dim path lights around it. Through the hiss of the wind in the trees and the gurgle of the pool, Jalen strained for the sound of dogs. He knew there were two. James Yager—JY—owner of the brick mansion and future Baseball Hall of Famer, was known nearly as well for his Rottweilers as his batting average. People even knew the dogs' names, Butch and Missy, and frequently the tweeted pictures of the Yankees' second baseman included JY's dogs.

As Jalen approached the batting cage, he peered around, looking for the baseballs that should be lying scattered about the cage floor. In the dark, he saw nothing. Panic choked him because he was there, in the dark night, for the balls. Jalen knew what James Yager did with those balls. Everyone knew that story. Cat had read the story aloud to him and Daniel right off her phone.

Once a week, the batting-cage balls, stamped with a

special Yankees logo and autographed by JY before he bashed them around inside the cage, were collected by the memorabilia team from Steiner Sports and sold online for a hundred dollars apiece to support the Yager Youth Foundation. It was the limited number of balls and the skid marks from JY's bat—proof that the star player had not only signed, but actually *hit* them—that gave them their value. Jalen needed ten of them, and that was all he'd take to sell and then use the money to pay the $990 fee required to join the Rockton Rockets summer travel team.

He crept closer, fretting about whether the balls would even be there.

He knew the Yankees were on the road today for a series with Toronto, and if the balls had been collected, there wouldn't be a new batch of them until next Monday at the earliest. Too late. The Rockets' sign-ups ended Saturday. If Jalen got left out, he'd spend his summer busing tables in the back dining room at the Silver Liner to pay for what batting-cage time he could get at the Pro Swing down in White Plains, and that just couldn't happen. The Rockets were 13U, the biggest transition in a young player's career. If he couldn't spend the summer getting used to the larger field, he'd get left behind, and he knew it.

He slipped his fingers into the mesh netting and pulled it taut so he could see more clearly into the cage. The floor was bare, but beside the faint outline of the pitching machine rested what might be a plastic bucket. Gone was the idea of scrabbling around the edges of the net, scooping up the ten balls he needed and flying away. He looked back up at the big brick house. Only a few of the windows glowed from within. He knew Yager wouldn't be home, but he had no idea who else might be in the house. A maid? A cook? Someone to watch the dogs?

Whatever the case, he saw no signs of life, and he heard no sounds of dogs. So, with trembling hands, he lifted the net and ducked underneath it. He flung the backpack off his shoulders and dashed across the concrete floor to the pitching machine. He banged his knee on the machine and cried out against his will. He didn't stop to see if anyone had heard, because it *was* a bucket, a big bucket.

And it was more than half-full of baseballs.

Two at a time he grabbed them, stuffing them into his pack, counting because he needed no less than ten and wanted no more. Jalen could justify ten because the Yager Youth Foundation said its mission was to help kids like him. When he first read about it online on the Rockton Public Library computer, he'd shaken his head in disbelief. He'd read the foundation's mission statement three times, looking for a trick or a mistake, because how could a dream like that really come true?

Carefully he'd filled out the request and submitted it. He even told his father about it. Every day after school and four times on the weekends he'd checked his e-mail at the library. When he heard nothing from the foundation, he began to e-mail them and call, but he got only electronic replies that requests would be processed in the order they were received and that while YYF did its very best to fulfill all requests, applicants should also seek other sources of funding.

Jalen waited and waited. For three weeks he waited before he decided that he'd have to take matters into his own hands. Cat and Daniel agreed. It was like destiny that Yager lived right next door to Cat's stepfather. And it was like destiny that Daniel knew all the paths through the woods, and the one spot where you could scale the wall and—unlike by the front gates—there were no security cameras.

They were simply speeding up the foundation's process. They all agreed that if JY knew about Jalen, he'd *want* his foundation to help. Even though Jalen shared the same zip code with some of the richest people on earth, he lived in a tiny house near the tracks. His clothes came from Walmart, if not Kmart. He had no mother, and his father worked long hours for very little money. Jalen had over-heard his second-grade teacher talking about him when she didn't know he could hear her. She'd told another teacher that Jalen and his father lived "hand to mouth." He'd looked that up. It meant you struggled with money, and that was pretty true.

"Underprivileged" was the word the foundation used, and Jalen suspected that he qualified. The other thing the foundation was looking for was kids with a passion for baseball. The foundation wanted to help them pursue that passion by providing money for equipment, uniforms, and yes, travel team fees. That was why Jalen felt only the slightest twinge of guilt as he stuffed the last ball into his backpack and zipped it tight.

He chuckled out loud as he crossed the concrete floor, heading for the net. He knew he was smiling. He could feel it. He felt as light as a balloon.

But his smile, and his optimistic feelings, came crash-ing down when a terrible sound pierced the windy night. A terrible sound.

The sound of dogs.

3

JALEN GRABBED THE NET AND FLUNG IT UP AND over, but too much slack remained, and he found himself tangled in its folds. The sound of bloodthirsty barking closed in on him fast. With his heart in his throat, his eyes detected two shadows streaking toward him. Jagged white teeth flashed in the dim glow of the pool. He couldn't get away, and he knew it.

Jalen struggled to get back inside the batting cage. His hands flew, casting the net up and away. He knew he had only another instant when he broke free, falling backward into the cage as the dogs hit the net. Up and down they leaped, casting themselves into the mesh like demons. If they hadn't been jumping so high, Jalen felt certain they could have burrowed their way underneath, but they were mad with rage and flinging themselves as high and as hard as they could, punching the netting before it flung them back into the grass.

Still, he didn't feel safe, and he wasn't.

Floodlights from the house exploded into the darkness. Swimming in bright light, the dogs cast huge shadows that rose and fell like waves. Jalen hugged himself in fear and felt the pork chop bones in his pocket. He fumbled with their plastic wrapping, pinched the end of one, and poked it through a hole in the net with trembling fingers. One of the dogs lunged and snatched it from his hand, leaving his fingers wet with slobber. Quickly he removed the other bone and stuck it out too. The second dog attacked it. The bone flew and the dog continued to roar, barking at Jalen like he wanted him dead.

"Butch! Missy!" a man's deep voice shouted from near the house.

Jalen felt his insides crumbling. He'd spent so much time worrying about not being on that travel team that he'd never considered the consequences of being caught. It came to him now like a hammer blow. He'd be sent away. His father had no money for a lawyer. The world would come crashing down on him, and he'd find himself in some kind of detention home for kid criminals. He'd heard about those places.

Suddenly the second dog stopped and sniffed the bone, then gobbled it up and began to chew, trotting over next to the other dog to hunker down beside it and eat. Except for the crackle and grind of teeth on pork bones, everything went eerily quiet. Jalen backed away, stepping softly to the other side of the cage. His eyes never left the dogs as he swept the net high up over his head and slipped free. Crabbing sideways so he could watch the dogs, he moved as quickly as he could without making a noise, because he knew someone was out there, somewhere in the shadows.

Relief flooded him as he approached the trees. Their shadows would swallow him whole, and he could let loose with an all-out sprint for the wall. The thought of Cat's beacon swelled his heart.

He took a final deep breath, turned his back on the dogs, and set off like a rocket.

He was two strides from the tree line when someone tackled him from behind.

4

HIS BODY THUMPED THE GROUND.

He gasped for breath, but none came. It felt like his chest would explode until finally a great gust of air filled his lungs, then left with a groan. Whoever had tackled him was big and strong and had Jalen by the collar with one hand as the other fished around in the backpack before Jalen was lifted off his feet and shoved toward the house.

"Little thief." The man's growl oozed with disgust, and he muttered to himself as he propelled Jalen forward. "Butch! Disgraceful."

The bigger Rottweiler looked up from his chop with perked ears before smacking his lips and returning to the bone.

The man seemed to be limping, and they were half-way to the house, now under the glare of the lights, when Jalen found his voice.

"Please, let me go," he begged.

"Please? You live in a town like this, and you *steal*?" The man stopped and turned Jalen around to get a look at his face, and Jalen realized the man was James Yager himself, which wasn't possible because the Yankees were in Toronto.

"Please, you're my favorite player. You're my hero."

"I'm your *hero*? That makes it worse, kid." The player frowned. "Stealing from me? I get that. I can handle that, but those baseballs . . . they're for kids. Did you know that? Of course you did, otherwise why are you even back here?"

The Yankees second baseman steered Jalen uphill.

Jalen had so much to say, but shame strangled him and not a single word could squeeze through its grip. When they reached the pool area, Yager led Jalen through the gate. They walked right past the glowing electric-blue pool and circled the house to the far side, where a five-car garage stood. Beyond that in the grass was a large shed in the shape of a barn. Yager opened a side door and deposited Jalen inside before stepping back and dialing his phone.

"Hello," Yager said into the phone after a brief pause. "Well, it isn't really an emergency . . . what? No, I can't call back tomorrow." The player looked at his phone, insulted. His tall frame cast a long shadow in the grass, and the frown on his face gave him a demonic look. "This is James Yager. I've got a kid I caught stealing. . . . Yeah, a kid. At my house . . . 4367 Old Post Road."

Yager turned his dark, almond-shaped eyes on Jalen to size him up. "I don't know. Ten? Twelve? Fourteen, I guess? What's the difference? Look, I've got to get going first thing in the morning, and I'd like to get some sleep, but someone's gotta come get this kid."

"Press charges?" Yager raised an eyebrow at Jalen. "I guess so. He was stealing, right? . . . No, I said it's not an *emergency*, but it can't wait until tomorrow. . . . *Okay,* then it *is* an emergency. Call it what you want, lady. Just get a cop over here and take this kid, right? Okay. Good. Thanks."

Jalen's stomach churned and rolled. He swallowed down bile, desperate not to throw up.

Yager held up the phone. "So, that's that, kid. You stay in there and don't mess anything up. You don't want to make this worse than it already is. Trust me."

Yager pulled the door closed with a rattle and Jalen stood in the dark, frozen in terror. He tried to calm his breathing and imagine that it was all just a crazy bad dream. As his eyes adjusted to the faintest light filtering in through a window on the far side of the shed, he detected dark, heavy shapes of lawn equipment and what had to be a tractor sitting hunched on the floor. The window gave him an idea: escape.

He tried the door handle, turning it quietly only to find that the door had been locked from the outside. He skirted the equipment and reached up for the window. It was too high.

Heart thumping, he shoved a tire beneath it, then another, which he stacked on top. With three tires stacked, he climbed up and fumbled with the latch until he heard a metal *bang* behind him.

Jalen spun.

5

FEAR EXPLODED IN JALEN'S BRAIN.

The shed door was flung open, and a small light danced in the entryway.

Images of his father and the police and Yager's stern warning cluttered his thoughts.

"Jalen?" Cat's hushed call filled the shed.

"Cat?" Jalen climbed down from the tires and hurried across the shed, bumping his shin on something and crying out.

"Shh! Come on." Cat waved her phone frantically, directing him outside.

Floodlights from above the garage doors now lit up this side of the house. On the ground were a crowbar and a broken lock. Jalen squinted in the light.

"Hey!" An angry shout came from the direction of the house. It was Yager.

Cat had Jalen's arm, and she dragged him around the shed into the shadows. They slipped through the trees, with Cat leading. Her firm grip was a comfort to Jalen, and she seemed to know exactly where she was going.

"Hey!" The shout behind them was more distant now.

Jalen glanced back. The glow of lights from the house barely seeped through the woods now, and a nervous giggle bubbled from his throat. "We did it. *You* did it."

They stopped, huffing. Cat looked at her phone. "It's not over yet. Come on."

She took off again, this time at a brisk march. Sticks and twigs snapped beneath them, muted by the blowing leaves above. They came to the stone wall and hugged it, keeping the wall to their right and the faint glow of Yager's mansion to their left until they reached the spot where Daniel waited on the other side. Up and over they went.

Daniel's dark eyes showed all their white. His voice was pitched high. "What the heck happened? Where've you been? I heard the dogs and the shouting, and then it's been so quiet I thought you were . . . I don't know. Hot sauce. Did you get them?"

Jalen shrugged the backpack off and unzipped it for his friends to see.

"Wow. You really did it." Daniel reached in and held a ball up to study in the light of Cat's phone. "Hot. Sauce."

"Yeah." Jalen didn't feel as excited or joyful as he'd expected. Being held captive by the major league player and having then escaped still seemed impossible. "I did, but I better get going. I'll be lucky if my dad's not home already. What time is it, anyway?"

Cat checked her phone before holding it up so they could all see: 12:37.

"Oh, wow. Daniel, get me back to the gates." Jalen zipped the backpack and shouldered it.

"Did he *see* you?" Daniel's eyes sparkled in the light of the phone.

"He caught me," Jalen said. "Cat sprung me from his shed or barn or garage or whatever it was. Now come on. I've gotta go."

Daniel nodded and started off down the trail, but turned and walked backward. "Wait. You *met* him? What was he like? Was he nice?"

"Daniel, he caught me stealing his baseballs." Jalen threw his hands up toward the swaying trees. "How could he be nice?"

"Did he look old?"

Jalen glanced at Cat, who walked beside him, then answered Daniel. "He didn't have gray hair or a cane, if that's what you mean."

"Thirty-five isn't old," Cat said.

"It is in sports." Daniel kept walking backward.

"He was limping. Daniel, *please*." Jalen clasped his hands. "We've got to move. My dad might already be home."

Daniel's face fell. He gave a serious little nod and took off at a jog. Jalen followed.

"What will you say?" Cat asked, chugging along right beside him. "If your father's really back?"

"I have no idea." Jalen felt a new surge of panic and picked up speed.

6

JALEN LEFT HIS FRIENDS AT THE GATES. ON HIS
way down Old Post Road into town, he saw a car turning
his way. He ducked behind a thick tree and watched a
police cruiser drive past. His heart felt like a bomb ready
to go off. When the car was gone from sight, he took off
at a full sprint, running like he was being chased, another
flicker of shadow in a windswept night until he hit the railroad tracks and paused because he couldn't go another
step until he caught his breath.

The Silver Liner Diner was dark and empty.

With its lights on, it was a gem. The front of the restaurant was a real dining car from the defunct Hudson
Railway. Its polished steel and sleek lines drew people's

attention, if not their business for lunch or dinner. Built onto the back was a bigger dining room and the kitchen that made the Silver Liner much more than a diner. As nice as the Silver Liner looked, it was on the wrong side of the tracks, and Jalen knew there was a long list of previous owners who'd run the restaurant into bankruptcy over and over again. His father always said that was because no one before had ever brought his work ethic to the place, or his love of food.

Jalen took off again, lungs burning and legs aching. He went straight down the tracks, praying his father was tired and moving slow. Past the station, he scrambled up a bank of weeds, climbed a rusty fence, fell, rolled, and popped up in a full run again. As he sprinted toward their house—the original tiny train station from the 1800s turned into cramped living quarters years ago after the new brick station had been built—he realized it too was dark. That meant his father was somewhere between the diner and home, walking on the path that circled the wetlands. Jalen's shortcut down the tracks might have saved him. If his father was home and knew Jalen was missing, the lights would be burning. If he wasn't home, he would be any second.

Jalen tiptoed up onto the back porch, used the single key he kept in his pants pocket, and eased the back door open. He heard the faint rattle of keys and saw his father's shadow through the window of the front door. Jalen pulled the back door softly behind him and stepped into the bathroom, closing it just as the front door creaked open and the lights went on. Jalen heard his father's footsteps heading for Jalen's bedroom. He struggled out of his clothes and jammed them, along with his backpack, beneath the sink.

"Jalen?"

Jalen cleared his throat and tried to sound sleepy. "In here."

He plunked himself down on the toilet just as the door swung open and his father's shadow appeared. Light from the hallway glinted off his shiny bald head and the wireframe glasses he needed to see.

"Why are you here? In the dark?" His father's Italian accent knew no bounds at home. In the diner, he tried to sound as American as he could, but at home his accent could get thick.

"I just woke up and . . . my stomach." Jalen froze, silent and waiting to see if the story would float.

His father nodded slowly. Jalen couldn't read his face in the shadow, but he'd heard the low growl that came from his father's throat before.

Jalen knew his dad was boiling with anger.

7

"THAT CALAMARI, SHE'S NO GOOD." JALEN'S
father struck the wall. "I tell that fishmonger she's not
fresh, and he tell me yes, she's a fresh, but now you stomach is no good, and I serve seven people that calamari
tonight . . . *mannaggia!*"

Jalen flushed the toilet and stood at the same time,
pulling up his underwear. "I think I'm okay now."

"Mannaggia!" His father thumped the wall again.

Jalen knew the Italian curse word was a mild one,
because he'd looked it up years ago. Still, it sounded bad
the way his father said it, and he rarely said it unless something was wrong either with Jalen or the Silver Liner, and
this time it was both. Jalen felt guilty about the fishmonger.

The stuffed calamari his father had served him for dinner in the diner's kitchen was delicious. But relief overcame his guilt because he was on his way to his bedroom now and had gotten out of some pretty tight spots tonight.

His father tucked Jalen into the narrow bed with a kiss on each cheek. Jalen lay still, listening to his father getting ready for bed. His eyes drifted to the top of his dresser, where a simple picture frame held the photograph of Jalen's missing mother. He couldn't make out the details in the dark, but he didn't have to. He could see it with his eyes closed. She was dark-skinned and beautiful, with big round eyes, full red lips, and a dazzling smile. Sometimes his father would take the picture down and simply drink in the sight of her before sighing and returning it to what Jalen considered a place of honor beside his all-star baseball trophy.

It was strange that Jalen didn't know more about her, but years ago he had concluded that that single picture seemed to be all his father could bear as the painful reminder of her absence. Jalen was convinced that was why it remained in his room instead of his father's. This way, his father only had to see it when he chose to, not as a constant reminder. While the details were few, Jalen did know she was a singer who had the chance to chase her dream, but for some mysterious reason, part of the deal was that she had to leave Jalen and his dad behind. Every time Jalen thought he'd worked up the courage to ask more about her and what had happened, he froze.

Through the paper-thin walls, Jalen heard the shuffle of feet from his father's room, then the sound of him lying down with a groan. The familiar squeal of bedsprings filled the darkness for a moment, and then everything was quiet. Only when he'd heard his father snoring for a good ten minutes did Jalen slip from bed and remove his clothes and backpack from beneath the sink. In the dark safety of his own bedroom, the baseballs now felt like gems from another planet. He put them out on the bed. Their value was so great—one thousand dollars—that Jalen's fingers trembled. He'd never held something so precious in his own hands and had certainly never possessed anything so valuable.

Now all he had to do was convert them to cash. He knew how: eBay. They'd go fast.

Jalen put the baseballs into his one overnight duffel bag and zipped it up tight—it was the safest, most secure place he could think of. Slipping it under his bed, he lay back down, exhausted and ready to sleep.

He took a deep, relaxing breath, then realized something. If Yager told the police, which Jalen knew he would, all anyone had to do was watch for someone selling ten James Yager–signed batting cage balls on eBay. He had a thousand dollars' worth of baseballs, but now he couldn't sell them.

His eyes shot open.

Sleep was suddenly a million miles away.

8

THE NEXT MORNING JALEN SAT DOWN ON THE BUS next to Daniel.

"Man, you look like junk." Daniel laid a hand on Jalen's shoulder.

"That's about right," Jalen said. "I think I dropped off sometime between three and four."

"Last night was insane." Daniel winced at the memory. "All's quiet this morning, though, and believe me, if there was any dirt flying, my mom would have it. Hey, I hope you'll be ready for tonight with those baggy eyes."

"Tonight." Jalen rubbed his eyes and sighed. "I almost forgot."

"How could you forget our *last* game?" Daniel's eyes sparkled.

"We're one and ten, Daniel. I'd rather forget this season. I mean, the Zappa Home Insurance Gators? Sounds like a disease. It *was* a disease."

"Yeah, but you're hitting .787, and I've got eight home runs." Daniel was always the optimist. Where most people saw dog poop, Daniel saw fertilizer for flowers.

"You think we stand a chance against Chris Gamble and the A's tonight?" Jalen studied his friend's face.

Chris Gamble had a rubber arm, and his dad was the same coach they'd play for on the Rockton Rockets, a winner. Coach Gamble was a former single-A player for the Phillies, and he had been stacking his Little League teams since T-ball.

"Seriously," Jalen said, "tell me the truth."

With complete sincerity, Daniel nodded. "Bro, that's why you *play* the game. If it was all about who did what before and numbers and all that, you'd never have to go out on the field. Everyone could just show up in uniform and shake hands and go home. What's wrong with you?"

"How can you fight crazy?" Jalen was talking about their own coach, Mr. Winkman, who had no idea how to coach baseball. Coach Winkman decided batting order and what positions everyone would play by drawing numbers out of a hat. What made it even harder was that Jalen *knew* how they could be ten times better than they were. When he saw the game, it was like one of those big problems he remembered from an advanced math test they'd given him in school. All the numbers were spread out over a space the size of his hand, but they just came together in one big, beautiful picture in his mind. Jalen knew what their lineup should be. He knew who should play what position and why. He even knew the pitches the batters would get. It all just *came* to him, and it hurt not to be able to use it.

"Well, you're batting cleanup tonight, and I'm five," Daniel said.

"Which means we won't get up until the second inning, and it'll probably be the only time we bat until the bottom of the fifth."

The bus pulled up outside the school, and they got off. Sun drenched the paving stones, and bright-green leaves danced on their stems above. Daniel marched alongside him and made a small O with his lips as he fished for something inside his backpack. "Someone could get hit by a pitch?"

"Come on, that's our strategy?"

"Chris Gamble is a maniac." Daniel stopped in the crowd of kids milling toward the front doors and held up a finger. "I'm going to do everything I can to win."

"What's that supposed to mean?"

"Psychological warfare." Daniel reached into his pack again and held up a bright-pink Post-it note on his pointer finger.

"What?" Jalen hurried after him.

"Watch and learn, amigo. Watch and learn."

9

CHRIS GAMBLE WAS NO ONE TO MESS AROUND

with. Even the eighth graders gave the bully space. He was big and barrel-chested, with arms so long his hands dangled by his knees. The hint of a mustache was already making itself known on his upper lip.

Daniel walked right up to him at his locker in the hall. "Ready for tonight?"

Chris ran his meaty hand over the bristles of his crew cut. "Ready to club some seals."

Chris's mouth fell open so Jalen could see his pink tongue as he roared with laughter.

"Well, we're gonna give it all we got." Daniel offered the firm nod of a true competitor, patted Chris on the back, and headed on his way.

Jalen followed and leaned close to whisper. "What was that about? You think that scared him? Upset him? Are you trying to friend him to death?"

Daniel was counting, silently bobbing his head, mouthing the numbers. When he got to ten, he pivoted around on one heel and headed back down the hall. Up ahead, Chris's giant form lumbered through the crowd like a ship through rowboats, but as he passed, people turned to watch and clamped their mouths to hold back laughter.

Jalen could now see the Post-it that Daniel had left behind on Chris's back. He quickened his pace to read whatever Daniel had written that amused everyone so much, but was careful not to get too close. Finally he could make it out.

SORRY 4 THE SMELL

I JUST FARTED

Jalen looked around at all the delighted faces. He burst into a laugh that he was half a second too late to contain. He looked at Daniel, who saw his face and laughed out loud. It was like breaking a dam: one crack, and the entire hallway exploded with laughter. Daniel and Jalen high-fived with glee.

From the corner of his eye, Jalen saw Chris spin around and gape at his classmates. "What? What's so funny?"

He spun around and around until one of his A's teammates, Dirk Benning, snatched the Post-it from his back and showed it to him.

Chris roared, crumpled the note, and headed right for Jalen.

10

THE FIRST DAY JALEN EVER MET CAT, SHE SHOWED

up just in the nick of time.

Jalen had been at the public library, using the computer to do research for a Revolutionary War project, when a bad burrito from the school lunch had taken its revenge. With sudden and vicious cramps twisting his gut, Jalen dashed for the single men's bathroom only to find it was locked. He knew there was another downstairs on the other side of the library, but Jalen doubted he could make it there without an accident.

He knocked and begged for entrance, only to hear a dull "It's being used" through the thick wooden door. Jalen strained his ears for sounds of a flush or something, hand washing, anything that would give him hope as he danced from one foot to the other. Suffering terribly, he began to calculate the odds of a wild dash downstairs when the door to the ladies' room across the hall swung open, and there stood the prettiest girl Jalen had ever seen. He was so tormented by the burrito that he didn't have enough pride to be embarrassed. She gave him a knowing look and wasted no time grabbing Jalen by the arm and steering him right into the ladies' room, where, before closing the door in his face, she told him, "Don't worry, I'll keep a lookout."

Jalen didn't need any more of an invitation, and a true disaster was averted. Afterward, he had realized he was trapped. He had no way of exiting without coming face-to-face with the pretty girl. He wanted to melt, but the horror of being *in* the ladies' room hadn't allowed him time to pause, and only a few moments later—after a thorough hand washing—he emerged with what he knew from the mirror was a cherry-red face.

"Uh . . . thanks."

"I've got an older brother," she said, then nodded at his T-shirt, "and us Yankees fans gotta stick together, through thick and thin."

Jalen looked proudly at the big NY letters on his chest. "Yeah. True." His eyes went to the LADIES sign on the door. "Pretty horrifying."

The pretty girl waved her hand. "Aww, you've been there before."

"No." Jalen was horrified.

"Sure," she said. "I mean when you were little. Moms take their kids in there all the time. No big deal."

Jalen stared at her for a moment. "No."

She laughed. "Don't lie."

She sounded like she was kidding, but the explanation just sprang from Jalen. "No, I don't have a mom."

"Oh." The girl's face fell, then brightened. "Hey, I don't have a dad. I mean, I have a stepdad, but trust me, no way does *he* count."

Jalen had no answer for that.

"Name's Catrina." She stuck out her hand, chomping on gum that had filled the air with peppermint. "But I like 'Cat.'"

In the brief instant before Chris Gamble grabbed two fistfuls of Jalen's shirt and shoved him into the lockers, that was what Jalen thought of: Cat, saving him.

Chris breathed something rotten through his fat lips into Jalen's face. The rancid odor caused him to blink, and when he opened his eyes, there she was.

Cat was tapping Chris on the shoulder. "Hi, Chris. What's wrong?" She spoke in a sweet, sisterly tone of genuine concern, piercing the boy ogre's rage.

Chris's eyebrows went up, and he turned his attention to Cat, although his grip didn't lessen in any way. Jalen still felt his toes dancing in the air and the metal vents of the locker scraping the knobs of his spine.

"Jokers is what's up." Chris snarled. "Jokers looking to get their teeth bashed in."

"Don't do *that*," said Cat. "You've got your last regular season game tonight. You don't want to mess that up. You gotta get used to jealousy, Chris. When you're a major league pitcher, people are going to be taking potshots at you all the time."

Chris's face softened. Cat knew right where his underbelly was and just how to scratch it. With her big eyes, long, straight nose, and high cheekbones, she was so pretty it didn't matter that her bulky sweatshirt was grass-stained and her jeans were torn at the knees. It almost made her prettier, like a flower bursting with color from a tangle of thistles and weeds.

"Yeah." Chris nodded and replanted Jalen against the lockers with a shove before letting go. "I know. You're right. Can't let the little rodents drag you down. Heh-heh."

"Come on." Cat angled her head down the hall. "You going to homeroom? Let's walk."

Chris turned to go; then, under his breath so no one else could hear, he threw one last punch. "You mutt."

And just like that, Chris was gone, lumbering along beside her, talking box scores from last night's games.

Jalen knew what Chris meant by the word "mutt." With most people it would mean you were a dog, and not in a good way. With Jalen, it meant he was biracial, half white and half black.

He clenched his fists and coiled his legs, preparing to launch himself at the other boy. He could strike him hard and fast, maybe even get in a knockdown punch, maybe even win the fight.

JALEN PAUSED AND THOUGHT ABOUT THE POTENTIAL

consequences of his actions.

He huffed and unclenched his hands. He dusted his shirt off and picked up his tumbled books.

"Here, let me help." Daniel picked up a notebook, still snickering over the success of his prank.

"Thanks a *lot*." Jalen ignored all the stares, and people began to filter toward their homerooms.

"I was gonna save you." Daniel's eyes sparkled.

"You and what army?"

"I was getting ready to chop him right in the fat part of his neck. Right here." Daniel pointed to a vulnerable spot between his own vertebrae. "One chop and they go down like a ton of bricks."

"This isn't the dojo." Jalen had all his books now, and he turned to go.

"Martial arts is for real. Don't test the will of kung fu."

"What does that even mean?" Jalen dismissed his friend with a wave of his hand.

He didn't see Cat until fourth period in science class, but when he did, she was all smiles. The three friends sat on stools along one side of a lab table waiting for their teacher.

"I hope you didn't have to invite Chris to your birthday party Saturday night." Jalen grinned. "That would be torture."

"He's not that bad, Jalen," she said.

Jalen made a face. "Ugh, those moles on his cheek?"

"He kind of reminds me of my brother, Austin," she said. "He'll be coming home from college soon."

Jalen felt a bit ashamed and wanted to change the subject. Certainly he didn't want to hear any more about how Chris wasn't that bad. "Well, you may have saved my life, but I'm not sure if it was enough to save my baseball career. His dad might just ban me from the Rockets."

"His dad's not gonna ban you from the travel team for sticking a note on his son's back. Anyway, I told him it wasn't you, and he believed me."

"It *wasn't* me." Jalen eyed Daniel, who got suddenly

interested in the homework sheet from the day before. "But that's not what I was talking about. I can't just sell those baseballs on eBay anymore. Someone could be watching."

"Hmm." Cat stared hard at her pencil before looking up. "You may be right." She removed the phone from her pocket and opened the browser. "By the way, here's why your favorite ballplayer—if he still *is* your favorite player—was home last night. Tweaked that bad ankle of his, and they wanted him to get an MRI and some hydrotherapy at the stadium. Meredith Marakovits tweeted that his condition is day to day."

"Why do you say *if* he's still my favorite player? He's James Yager, maybe the greatest second baseman ever. Why wouldn't he be?"

"Well, now that you met him up close." Cat popped her gum. "I mean, he imprisoned you in his barn, and he's on the downside of his career. Maybe at the end with that ankle."

Daniel had obviously been listening, because he put a hand on Jalen's shoulder and said, "This guy is loyal like a soldier. You can't shake Jalen if he's on your side. That's just not how Jalen rolls."

Jalen looked at his friend, wondering if he was talking about Yager or himself, and then he decided both. "So, now what do I do?" he asked Cat. "About the baseballs? I couldn't even sleep last night, worrying."

Cat clenched her fists. "I wish that stupid stepfather of mine . . ."

"Don't go there, Cat."

"Okay, you're right." Cat's frown rebounded, and she held up a finger. "Hey, a dealer. We can sell them at that memorabilia shop in Valhalla. We can take the train down after school and be back before dinner and your game."

"I didn't think of that. But do you think they'll give me a hundred apiece for them?"

Cat set her jaw the way she did when she was lining up a penalty kick. "There's only one way to find out."

12

THE TRAIN RIDE DOWN AND BACK TO VALHALLA

got Jalen only five hundred dollars, and the sports memorabilia dealer, a heavy blond hairy guy chewing on a green
unlit cigar, told Jalen he was lucky to get that. They rode
in grim silence back to Rockton until Daniel said, "Can you
believe that guy *sells* dirt?"

"Yeah, but think about what happened on that dirt." Cat's
voice was low and serious. "Rivera's six hundred and second save? Jeter's three thousandth hit? Teixeira's eleventh-
inning homer in game two of the ALDS? How about Matsui's
six RBIs and the Yankees winning their twenty-seventh title?
It's not something my stepfather would pay for, that's for
sure, but I can't say I wouldn't love to have some. . . ."

"Yeah . . ." Daniel got a faraway look as he stared out the window. "Like your own piece of history, right?"

Jalen didn't join in. He couldn't even think about it. He was too dejected about the fact that he was still $490 short for his travel team.

His friends sensed his mood, but when they stepped off the train at the Rockton platform, Daniel clapped his hands together one time like a firecracker. "I got it."

"You got what?" Jalen couldn't believe how glum he felt for a kid with a fat roll of twenty-dollar bills in his pocket.

"Coach Gamble loves to win, right? I mean, he's all about winning." Daniel nodded, urging them to follow along.

"No doubt about that," Cat said.

"Like a dog loves a bone," Jalen said. "Like a pirate loves gold."

"So, amigo, you gotta shine tonight like you never shone before." Daniel clapped a hand on Jalen's shoulder. "Make him *hungry* to get you on the Rockets. Make him desperate. Make him—"

"Give you a price break." Cat snapped her fingers and looked from Jalen to Daniel. "And people say you're not smart."

"What? *Who?*" Daniel asked.

Cat ignored him. "This could work. I'm sure they build

some fat into those entry fees, keep a rainy-day fund or something. But it's true, you gotta make Mr. Gamble *hungry*."

"How?" Jalen asked, even though he thought he knew.

"We gotta beat their pants off!" Daniel pumped a fist into the air.

Jalen's face sank. They stood as much chance of winning as Jalen did of having his long-lost mother show up out of the blue.

"No." Cat shook her head. "You don't have to beat *them*, but Jalen has to beat *him*."

Jalen knew exactly who she meant.

The best pitcher Rockton Little League had seen in three decades.

He had to beat Chris.

13

THE ONLY THING LONGER THAN COACH WINKMAN'S
mustache was his hair. He wore a faded SAVE THE PLANET
T-shirt, jeans, and Birkenstocks. The only thing suggest-
ing he was a baseball coach was the bright-orange cap
he wore, just like his players, with a fat green gator's face
on it. Jalen heard the owner of Zappa Home Insurance
was a bonkers University of Florida fan who had insisted
they use his team's colors and mascot if he agreed to be a
sponsor. And the team played as horribly as they looked.

Thankfully, it was Jalen's turn this game to play shortstop. Daniel, their best pitcher by a landslide, was stuck out
in right field and batting ninth, despite going yard more
than any kid in the league. Jalen huffed at the thought, but

as he jogged out onto the field, he comforted himself with the notion that with Bobby Reynolds on the mound, he was apt to have a lot of action in the field. Behind his back, the rest of the kids called him Bobby Meatball. That's what he threw. Meatballs. The last time he pitched, the game got called either for darkness or the mercy rule—Jalen had never gotten a straight answer from their coach—but they lost 23–1.

With balls flying around like mosquitoes, Jalen felt sure he'd have a chance to make Coach Gamble drool, and he didn't have to wait long. After Reynolds walked his first two batters, the third A's player flubbed a pop-up that was going to drop nearly on top of the pitching mound. When the ball reached its high point, Jalen realized Bobby Meatball wasn't moving on it, but instead was watching like it was some shooting star. Jalen bolted toward the mound and scooped the pop-up with a shoestring catch.

"Make sure you call for those." Coach Winkman spoke in a loud but polite voice and clapped his hands enthusiastically. "Jalen? You need to call for it if you're going to field someone else's ball."

Jalen tried to keep his blood from boiling; he wanted to shout that if Bobby hadn't stood there like a statue, he would have been happy not to bust a gut to make the play. Of course, Jalen would never do that. First, it would be mean. Second, he was glad he'd gotten to make a play like that.

When Chris stepped up to the plate as the cleanup batter with two on, Jalen saw his stance and moved so close to second base, he could smell the tuna fish on the runner's breath. Jalen glanced at the dugout, worrying about Coach Winkman moving him back, but the coach was looking at his iPhone.

Bobby lobbed the ball over the plate, and Chris smashed it. The frozen rope nearly took Bobby's head off, but luck and just the hint of a reaction saved his hash. Jalen launched himself into the air, snagged the liner, and darted at the runner, tagging him and turning two before the kid could even start heading back to the base.

Jalen trembled with joy as he jogged to the dugout. Daniel caught up to him and slapped him silly. "You da *man!*"

Jalen brushed past his friend, embarrassed that the small crowd was clapping for him. He did look up, though, to catch Cat's eye in the stands. They pointed at each other the way they always did, her to let him know she was watching, and him to let her know he appreciated it. His other teammates clapped his back as well, and even Coach Winkman knew enough about baseball to be impressed. He wiggled a pinky finger in his ear and chuckled. "Wow.

Some play. And you weren't even in the right place, Jalen. Heh-heh, better to be lucky than good, right?"

Jalen bit his lip. He couldn't even explain how he knew that ball was going down the middle of the field, he'd just known that it was. Something about Chris's feet? His posture, maybe? His grip? Maybe all of the above? Jalen didn't know how he knew the things he knew about the game, only that he *knew* them, and he was rarely wrong.

He pushed that from his mind and turned his attention to the gunshot cracks of Chris's pitches hitting the catcher's mitt. Chris threw mostly cheese with his big arm, but even Jalen had to admit that the kid had a heck of a three-finger changeup. On his last warm-up pitch, Chris threw a curve that dropped right over the lower corner of the plate. After it hit Dirk Benning's catcher's mitt, Chris smiled at the A's dugout, and Jalen saw Coach Gamble, a bear of a man, standing there with his arms crossed, giving his son a big thumbs-up.

Jalen swallowed hard. Most pitchers didn't throw a curve in Little League even if they could, but Chris was so big, Jalen had to wonder if the normal rules didn't apply. Either way, it'd be hard to do what Cat said. Making plays in the field was one thing. Defeating a pitcher like Chris was a whole other level.

Chris sat the first three runners down with just ten

pitches, then Jalen and his team watched Meatball give up three runs before they could end the inning. It was the bottom of the second inning when Jalen stepped up to the plate. He was really nervous, more than normal, more than he should be without knowing why. Chris gave him a mean smile.

Jalen knew what was coming before it came. It was why he'd been nervous. Still, he had a hard time processing it because he didn't think it was possible, even as Chris went into his windup.

When Jalen saw the ball coming at him, he knew—possible or not—it was true.

His heart froze.

14

JALEN HIT THE DECK.

Chris had thrown what was meant to be a bean ball right at Jalen's head.

Because he'd known it was coming, Jalen saved himself a concussion. The ball went over Dirk and the umpire as well. Jalen was facedown in the dirt.

"Hey!" the umpire shouted, and pointed at Chris. "Another one of those, and you're gone!"

"It was a wild pitch!" Coach Gamble burst from the dugout, his twisted face as red as a fire engine. He was a bigger version of his son. Same three prominent moles on his face. Same huge frame slumped and long-armed like an ogre, only much hairier than Chris. His roar was impressive, but the ump didn't back down.

"You know and I know your son doesn't throw wild pitches." The umpire glowered.

Jalen heard Dirk snickering at him from behind his catcher's mask, but he got to his feet and dusted himself off. "It's fine. I was crowding the plate."

The adults both looked at him in surprise.

"Uh . . ." The ump lost some steam.

"See?" Coach Gamble pointed at Jalen. "He was crowding."

"Okay, well." The ump adjusted his mask. "I don't want to see it again. I'm serious."

Coach Gamble looked at Jalen with just a flicker of appreciation before he shouted to his son, "Keep it down, Chris!"

Chris couldn't help smirking, but he covered it quickly with his glove and nodded that he understood. Jalen stepped into the batter's box and knew he'd see a fastball, right down the pipe. He did, swung, and missed.

"Strike!"

Jalen stayed in the box. He knew he'd get more heat and down the middle. It came. He swung and nicked it foul into the backstop.

"Strike two!"

Jalen stepped out, then watched Chris, who took a moment, searched the bleachers to find where Cat was sitting, and flashed a smile. In that moment, Jalen knew exactly what he was going to get. Chris wanted to bean him with the first pitch because of the note on his back in school. Even if Cat had calmed him down, he wanted revenge, and now he intended to strike Jalen out in style, showing off for Cat . . . with his changeup.

And that was a pitch Jalen *knew* he could hit.

He stepped into the box.

Chris wound up.

In it came.

15

JALEN SMASHED IT.

He took off down the first base line but slowed to a jog halfway to the bag. That ball was gone. Jalen bit his lip to keep from laughing out loud. He wanted to impress Chris's dad with his abilities, not stick out because he was some hot dog. He jogged the bases, crossed home plate, and accepted his teammates' high fives. Daniel hugged him and lifted him and spun him around.

"I didn't win the World Series," Jalen said.

"No, but I bet you got yourself a spot on the Rockets!" Daniel knocked off Jalen's cap to mess his hair. "He'll probably pay *you* to join. Hot *sauce!*"

Jalen was happy, but he didn't feel the certainty or the

joy that Daniel felt. Daniel tended to get overexcited, but Jalen had spent a lifetime not having enough money for things. He'd wasted a lot of time hoping that somehow, something would happen that would let him get whatever it was he wanted anyway. So he knew firsthand that life just didn't go that way, and he was far from certain it would go his way now.

They lost the game 17–1. Jalen had only one other at bat and punched a grounder down the first base line for a single, but he had a second double play as well as several other highlights in the field. When they shook hands, Chris ignored him. When Jalen looked hopefully into Coach Gamble's face for a sign of respect, or even recognition, he got nothing at all. The enormous coach's black eyes peered from beneath eyebrows that looked like electrocuted caterpillars, thick and wild. Black wires of hair sprouted from his nose and even from his ears. He lumbered past, muttering, "Good game," but anyone could see that his mind was someplace a million miles away.

Doubt screwed Jalen's stomach into a knot that remained only to tighten even more the next time he saw Coach Gamble's face.

The coach showed up at the diner bright and early Saturday to finalize Jalen's registration with the Rockets. It would be the first time the coach would hear about Jalen and Cat's price-break plan. The strategy was to spring it on him and maybe get him to say yes. Now the idea didn't seem so great, because Jalen felt certain that Coach Gamble had no love for surprises.

16

JALEN SQUIRMED UNDER THE GAZE OF COACH
Gamble's eyes studying him. The coach's thick, pale lips
turned downward, making part of Jalen wish he'd never
tried to join the man's team in the first place.

The three of them—Jalen, his dad, and the coach—sat
in the corner booth of the Silver Liner.

"Wait, you got the money, or you don't got the money?"
Coach Gamble raised the brim of his Rockets cap with a
thumb to better assess Jalen's dad now.

"Sure we got the money." Jalen's dad tapped two fingers
on the stack of bills before pushing them a little closer to
Coach Gamble across the table. "This is the money right
here. Jalen, he work a long time to get this. The snow, she

melt, and my son get all the golf balls in the woods. Then he sell the golf balls to pay you the money."

Jalen felt a pang of guilt at the sound of the story he'd told to his father, explaining the money. He'd focused really hard on the part about selling "balls" and not saying what kind of balls but that he'd found them in the woods, which was also sort of true. Jalen didn't lead his father anywhere close to the real truth in his explanation, but he hadn't outright lied either.

"That's a lot of golf balls, but this isn't *all* the money you need, Mr. DeLuca." Coach Gamble's face was growing more sour by the second. "I don't run a charity."

"*Who's* a charity?" It was Jalen's dad's turn to scowl. His back stiffened, and the wrinkles of his bald forehead were too numerous to count.

They were in dangerous territory, as Jalen feared they would be, because his father would go without food or clothes rather than ask for charity.

"The fee is nine hundred ninety dollars, not five hundred." Coach Gamble started to collect his paperwork and put it back into the open briefcase he'd laid out on the table. "Today is the last day of sign-ups. I've got two other kids wanting to join and only one spot left. I came here first because your son's got some game, but it ain't no charity."

"No. She's no charity." Jalen's father glowered and stood. "And nobody's asking for no charity."

Jalen watched his whole career crumbling in front of him. He'd never been certain about Cat's hopeful price-break plan, but one of the things that had come out of several sleepless nights this past week was an alternate plan. It was a crazy scheme, but it was all he had, and he wasn't going to go down without exhausting every possibility.

"Wait," Jalen said.

They both looked at him like he'd lost his mind.

17

JALEN SET HIS JAW. "COACH GAMBLE, THIS IS ALL my fault. I want to play on your team really, really bad, and I knew I didn't have enough, but my dad has this diner and I *know* you buy a lot of food for the team, sandwiches for the bus rides, and . . . and I heard you do a party at the end of the season and, well . . . why couldn't my dad do that stuff to make up the difference? He could probably *save* you money."

Both men looked at Jalen in surprise. Jalen begged silently, staring hard into his father's pale-blue eyes, which—even when he was mad—twinkled with kindness and laughter. There was a long, uncomfortable silence, but Jalen stayed strong, and finally his father's scowl melted into a grin, and he put a hand on Jalen's shoulder. "My son. How about my son? What do you think, Coach? I make you the food. You make-a me the baseball player. . . ."

Father and son turned to see how Coach Gamble would respond.

The coach's face was like a glacier, cold and unmoving, and Jalen wasn't hopeful. He could hear Coach Gamble's heavy breathing, a slow wheeze moving in and out of his enormous nose.

Finally he licked his lips like a Saint Bernard and grumbled, "What kind of sandwiches?"

"What you like?" Jalen's dad glowed with delight. "Eggplant parmesan? Prosciutto with melon? How about some nice salmon with capers and lemon and . . ."

"For sandwiches?" The coach reared back.

"Yes, is the best." Jalen's dad gave a nod of complete certainty.

Coach Gamble raised his thick eyebrows and gave a look around. "That's what you serve in a place like this?"

Jalen's father chuckled. "She's the Silver Liner. Like in you pockets. She's-a rich and she's elegant."

"Clouds have silver linings. This place says diner, which in my experience has sandwiches."

"For people that like a diner, I got the eggs and the bacon

and a cheeseburger make you mouth water." Jalen's dad brought his fingers to his lips. "And fries. And a shake. But people who know? They come for the homemade recipes from the *nonna* and sit in the back, where I got the dining room. Stuffed calamari. Steak Florentine. Fregnacce. Eggplant rollatini. *Frutti di mare.* And the pasta I make myself, every morning."

"Can you just do like . . . ham and cheese?" Coach Gamble asked in a gruff voice. "Maybe some turkey? Normal stuff. You know, like Quiznos."

Jalen watched the joy slip away from his father's face. His dad had told him point blank one time that if Jalen ever ate a sandwich from Quiznos, it would be an insult to his ancestors. But his father knew what was at stake, and he swallowed his pride. "Coach, you put my son on your team, and I make you any sandwiches you want."

Coach Gamble digested that news for a few moments before continuing. "And the party . . . that could be just spaghetti and meatballs. Maybe a salad."

"Coach, I cook you a *feast*."

"No. Just spaghetti. Meatballs. Tomato sauce. Nothing fancy. Bread and butter. You can do that too, right?"

"I . . ." Jalen's dad held up a finger. His mouth fell open, but no words came out until he regrouped and nodded vigorously. "I give you just what you want, Coach."

"Good." Coach Gamble stood up. "It's a deal. Sign here. Sign here. Sign there."

Jalen's dad signed and the coach gathered up his things before they all stood up. The two men shook hands, and Coach Gamble laid a big paw on Jalen's shoulder. "I liked how you played Wednesday night. You played good, but you can be even better. That's what it'll take to be a Rocket."

"I will, Coach."

Coach Gamble pressed his lips tight with doubt. "Okay. We'll see. We start Monday at the big field in Simon Park. The schedule's in the materials I left you."

Jalen knew there were two Little League play-off games today, with the championship tomorrow evening, so Monday made sense.

"Coach, good luck in the play-offs." Jalen wanted to make a good impression, but the coach only snorted.

"We don't need luck. Luck is for weaklings. Welcome to the Rockets." With a short nod, he left them standing there.

18

AS JALEN AND HIS DAD WATCHED THE ENORMOUS
man lumber out of the diner, Jalen's dad put an arm
around him and spoke in a whisper. "Welcome to baseball
Rockets."

Jalen worked hard all day in the kitchen, helping
his dad, washing dishes, taking the garbage out to the
Dumpster behind the train station. At first he seemed
to be floating. His cheeks began to ache from the constant smile. He'd dreamed and hoped for so long that
he could become a Rocket. He *needed* to be a Rocket.
He couldn't afford to miss the next and possibly most
important step as a young player—the transition to the
big field—if his dreams of baseball greatness were to

be fulfilled. Still, he had never been entirely certain he would pull it off.

As the day wore on, though, he came back down to earth. The balloon of joy in his chest sprang a leak. And, late in the day, gravity seemed to be turned up to its highest level. It took a focused effort just to pick his feet up off the floor. Then, as he was washing out a sink his father had used to clean some octopus, a fire broke out on the stove.

"Mannaggia!"

Jalen hurried over, but by the time he got there, his dad already had the great burst of flames under control. Only a small pool of fire rolled across the stove top, still dangerous, but not alarming.

"Go back, Jalen!" his father shouted at him as he grabbed the big frying pan with both hands and shuffled over to the sink, where he cooled everything with water. Steam hissed as it escaped, and his father turned his bright-red face away from it, still holding on to the pan.

"Dad! Your arm." Jalen reached for his father.

"No, no, she's okay. She's okay." His father waved Jalen off, but he realized his dad wasn't talking about the long, angry burn on his arm from the pan. He was talking about the octopus he'd saved from the fire.

Suddenly Jalen wanted to cry. Cry because he'd stolen and cry because he'd lied to his father, the man in front of him grinning with joy because he'd saved thirty dollars' worth of food from the fire. His father glowed with goodness, kindness, love, honesty, and hard work. It made Jalen think of his mother, because surely he was more like her than his father, a person to sneak about and disappear without warning.

Thinking of his mother made him want to ask about his mother, but he just couldn't do that. It wasn't worth the look of discomfort on his father's face. In times past, when the subject of his mother had come up, his father's face would flicker with joy only to be quickly clouded over with visible pain. Whatever the story was, Jalen could only assume that a mother who'd leave her son was someone entirely undependable. Someone thinking of herself before others.

Jalen suddenly felt more than heavy. He felt sick because wasn't that who he was? His story about the golf balls made him realize that maybe there would have been a way for him to get the money he needed to play *without* taking the baseballs. His father never would have done that. His father would have done it the honest way or not at all.

He remembered just last week when his father got angry with a waitress who bragged about selling the bronzino special, an expensive whitefish from the Mediterranean Sea, by telling the customer that the fish was freshly caught. Jalen's dad had offered the fish special for several days already and he'd marched out into the diner to talk to the customer.

"She's *not* fresh." Jalen's dad stood over the surprised customer. "The bronzino, she's four days old. She's good, but she's not fresh."

"Uh, okay." The customer was a man in a wrinkled suit with a tie he'd loosened after a long day. "I'll have a cheeseburger instead."

A $7.99 cheeseburger instead of the $23.99 bronzino special.

That was his father.

"Jalen! Jalen!"

Jalen was startled from his recollection by his father's cry for help cleaning up the spilled grease that had spattered over everything within four feet of the stove, and he got down on his hands and knees, keeping his head down and wiping away a tear so as not to upset his dad.

All afternoon, people had dripped into the diner like a leaky faucet. There never was a surge of business that day, or any day Jalen ever knew about. His dad talked regularly about the need to advertise, but the problem was the cost. His father spent too much money at the market, insisting on buying only the very best ingredients. That meant—when business was slow, or people just didn't order the specials—good food often went to waste, and it seemed his father could never quite catch up. Certainly he didn't have the spare funds to invest in a radio or print ad campaign for the Silver Liner.

Jalen worked even harder than normal because he was going to Cat's birthday dinner in the evening, and he wanted to do as much as he could if he was going to abandon his father on a Saturday night. It wasn't going to be a grand party—like someone who only knew where Cat lived might expect. Her stepfather was very rigid when it came to spending money, especially on things for Cat. To hear her talk, you'd think she was no better off than Jalen or Daniel. Even though there were some things that let you know she was rich—like her up-to-date iPhone and her fancy bedroom and her swimming pool—there was a limit on all kinds of things that surprised Jalen. He knew Cat had a meager budget for clothes and school supplies, and the only books she was allowed had to be borrowed from the library. Still, Cat said her mom promised a "surprise."

After saying good-bye to his dad, Jalen trudged down the gravel drive that led to their house, thinking about how none of it made sense. What good was having a big old mansion and a two-hundred-acre estate when your stepdaughter couldn't buy a book? Jalen washed his face and hands before changing into his good clothes, a stiff white dress shirt with black slacks that barely reached his ankles. He tried on the dress shoes, but they didn't come close to fitting.

With a sigh, he slipped on his broken-down sneakers and eyed the box of homemade cannoli on the kitchen counter. Cat had said absolutely no presents, but Jalen's dad made him promise to bring the cannoli, so he picked up the box and set out, wondering what the big birthday surprise was. He picked up Daniel at the stables.

Daniel looked uncomfortable too, in a powder-blue button-down shirt and dress pants, but with deeply polished black shoes that fit his feet. Daniel nodded at the box under Jalen's arm. "Cat said no presents. What's that?"

"Just cannoli." Jalen nodded at the clump of wildflowers in Daniel's hand. "What's that?"

"Just flowers. Come on. I've been waiting. Cat's mom told her that her birthday surprise would knock our socks off."

"How could something free be so good?" Jalen asked under his breath as they circled the giant mansion to go in the back way. "You know her stepfather doesn't let her mom spend any money."

"I have no idea." Daniel shrugged. "The guy is nuts."

Jalen rang the bell, and they heard it sound inside like an electric buzzer. "And why would her present knock *our* socks off?"

Daniel licked his hand and smoothed down the hair on his head. "I have no idea about that, either. Her stepdad's in London or something, so maybe her mom *did* spend money, but stop worrying about it, because we're about to find out."

The door swung open suddenly, and Cat's face was aglow.

19

"WE'VE BEEN WAITING FOR YOU GUYS." CAT waved them in. "My mom said she wasn't going to show me what my surprise is until you were here. Come on. Jalen, you wiped your feet enough, come on."

"I'm trying to be polite." Jalen's face warmed in embarrassment with the attention to his feet and sneakers.

"And my mom said no presents."

"It's just cannoli." Jalen handed her the box. "Homemade."

"Here." Daniel handed her the clump of flowers. "These aren't anything either. Just flowers."

"You guys are awesome." Cat's eyes sparkled, and she took both the cannoli and the flowers, then led her friends around a corner, up some stairs, and down a long hallway to an enormous wood-paneled dining room complete with a crackling fire at one end. Silver glinted in the light of a hundred candles. On one end of a very long table, five places had been set with multiple forks, knives, and spoons.

A butler wearing a black bow tie stood as still as a statue but flicked his eyes at Daniel in silent warning when Cat's mom entered the room.

"They're here?" Cat's mom had a deep, silky voice. She reminded Jalen of a storybook queen. There was something almost frightening about her beauty, with her high cheekbones, delicate nose, and glossy black hair. "Welcome, boys. Sit, please. Jalen, you're next to Cat. Daniel, you're over on this side with me. You can be my date."

Jalen was confused. Cat's brother, Austin, was at school, so he'd assumed that the fifth place was for her stepfather and that Daniel was simply mistaken about London.

"Oh, Cat." Cat's mom frowned. "Wearing jeans? Cat, look how nicely your friends are dressed."

"Clothes aren't important, Mother." Cat flashed her smile. "And it's my birthday."

"Yes, it is. Sit, everyone." Cat's mom had striking blue eyes like Cat's, only they were somehow sad. The light in them reminded Jalen of a painting he'd seen in a library book once of a small, nearly hopeless campfire beneath an enormous dark sky. Cat's mom slipped into her place, and they all followed her lead. Then she reached across the table and gripped Cat's hand, giving it a little shake. "You know I always tell you the day you were born was the best day of my life, Cat."

Cat blushed and looked down.

"Well, it's true." Her mom drew Cat's eyes up from the plate with a beckoning finger until they were looking at each other and smiling like they shared a secret. "And I know how you and your friends all love baseball."

Her mom giggled and looked around at them before returning to Cat. "And especially Yankees baseball."

Cat nodded enthusiastically. Jalen and Daniel followed her lead.

"So . . ." Cat's mom cleared her throat and gave the butler a nod.

He turned and disappeared through a side door.

"For your twelfth birthday"—her mom looked expectantly at the door—"I've arranged for you and your friends to have dinner with . . ."

They all turned their attention toward the side door now.

It swung open, and Jalen thought he might throw up.

"J-aaaaa-ames *Yager!*"

20

THE PRO BALLPLAYER LOOKED LIKE HE'D BEEN HIT
with a brick.

Jalen's mind was already out the door, flying like the wind, and halfway to Old Post Road, but terror chained his legs to the chair.

"You!" Yager pointed at Jalen. "You're that kid. . . ."

Cat's mom looked at Jalen in alarm.

Cat flew out of her seat and took the ballplayer by the arm. "The kid who's e-mailed your foundation website more than a hundred times. I know, I know, Mr. Yager, but I'm the one who told him you have to be persistent, so it's really on me and maybe—since it's my birthday—you'll forgive and forget. Forgive and forget is what my mom says all the time."

Yager looked at Cat like she was crazy and tried to gently pull his arm free, but Cat didn't let go. She was talking fast and forcefully and leading him toward his chair. "I am so, *so* happy you're here! James Yager. Mother, you're just amazing. The very *best*.

"Mr. Yager, these are my best friends in the whole world. I love them like brothers, don't I, Mother? Don't *we* love them?"

Startled and looking embarrassed, Cat's mom gaped at her daughter. "I . . . yes. You do. Yes, *we* do. These boys are wonderful, James. I certainly hope Jalen's persistence wasn't an annoyance. I'm sure you get hundreds of e-mails a day, but . . . but how did you recognize Jalen from an e-mail?"

"I meant a *message*, Mother." Cat's face turned red, but she recovered with a jingle of laughter. "I meant a *message* on Facebook. *That's* how he sent the messages, but I thought you'd understand it better if I just said 'e-mail.'"

Cat's mother looked at James, who now stood beside the chair at the head of the table, wearing dark jeans and a brown herringbone blazer.

"I can't keep all this social media straight." Cat's mother forced a laugh. "Can you, James? Twitter or Flitter or Snapchap or Instant Grahams or whatever it is they do?"

"I, uh . . . I actually have someone who does all that for me." Yager was still off balance, but seeming to soften. His scowl had eased into a mild frown "But I do know what you mean. It's . . ."

They all appeared uncomfortable waiting for him to finish, but no one was more on edge than Jalen.

"It's"—Yager began to snap his fingers in an attempt to recover his thoughts—"changing all the time, I guess."

Then the Yankees star smiled. "But it's good to meet—is it Jalen?"

"Jalen DeLuca," Cat's mom said.

"Right. It's good to meet Jalen DeLuca in person. Wow, what a small world."

Still looking unsettled, Yager took his seat.

"Really, it's not small at all." Cat opened her hands and raised them toward the heavy wood-paneled ceiling, speaking in a singsong voice. "We live with my stepdad— who has more money than God—and he lives next to *you*—a very famous baseball player who also makes a lot of money—and we're all just . . . just the kids in the neighborhood."

"The neighborhood?" Yager raised an eyebrow.

"Daniel's family works and lives at Tipton," Cat's mom explained. "And Jalen lives in town. His father owns the Silver Liner. Have you been to the Silver Liner? It's excellent."

"Owns the Silver Liner? Hmm." The player nodded

slowly. "So, what're we having? What's the birthday girl's favorite?"

"Lamb chops." Cat beamed, and Jalen wondered if it was because of lamb chops, or that she'd successfully prevented Yager from spilling the story to her mom about Jalen stealing baseballs.

"Oh, good," Yager said. "I'm a big fan of lamb chops."

There was a moment of awkward silence before Daniel spoke up. "So, JY, did you get paid to be here?"

"Oh!" Cat's mom let loose a small laugh.

"Daniel!" Cat scowled. "That's not polite."

"Well, I figured . . . players get paid for appearances, don't they? You read that all the time."

"James is a friend," Cat's mom said. "I saw him at a fund-raiser for the arts, and we talked about being neighbors and his foundation and . . . well, my husband and I wanted to make a contribution and help out."

"See?" Daniel sat straight, bright-eyed.

"See what?" Cat flared her nostrils. "They're talking about charity work. They're friends."

"Yeah, no. No one paid me." Yager said it like it was final.

Daniel slouched, and salad was served by the butler and a young woman with a solemn look.

"Well, I bet all you big Yankee fans have about a

million questions for Mr. Yager." Cat's mom looked around hopefully.

Jalen studied his fork and poked at a thin ribbon of carrot.

"Cat?" her mom asked.

"Um . . . yeah. Well, how's your ankle?" Cat asked.

Yager picked up his fork and nodded. "Good. Better every day. I'll be back in the lineup next week."

"Do you feel old?" Daniel peered from beneath his thick cap of black hair, his dark-brown eyes drilling for information.

"Daniel!" Cat glared.

"What? That's all they talk about on the MLB Network." Daniel sulked a bit, and muttered under his breath, "Hot sauce."

Yager actually laughed. "Yeah, you know, I do feel old."

Daniel's cheeks glowed, revealing a white-toothed grin. "Must be hard. Especially with that Jeffrey Foxx coming in with his fancy-pants bow ties 'cause he's some genius or something. Who needed a new GM? We were fine."

"They call him a genius because he's a numbers whiz, and he is," Yager said, "but I don't like his bow ties either."

"My dad says he's not as smart as he thinks he is." Daniel was on a roll now and comfortable enough to stuff some salad in his mouth and keep talking. "My dad says the game ain't all about numbers. My dad says it's about *heart*."

"Your dad's a smart man," Yager said, taking a drink from the crystal water glass in front of him before digging into his salad. "But . . . Foxx is our GM, so . . ."

Yager suddenly looked thoughtful. Then he brightened up. "But it's your birthday, Cat. Your mom said you're a huge Yankees fan. What can you tell me about CC Sabathia?"

"Well, I do know that in his first Yankee season he won nineteen. And then he won three postseason games that year." Cat stuffed some salad into her smile. "He was big-time."

Yager was obviously impressed, and that let Jalen breathe a small sigh of relief because he could tell that the star player wasn't going to out him, not during Cat's birthday dinner, anyway. Still, Jalen couldn't bring himself to speak, and he only stole quick glances at Yager, even though just a few days ago it would have been a dream come true to sit at the table with the famous ballplayer.

Dinner actually went by in a blink. Cat and Daniel loosened up plenty, and JY was relaxed and joking with them by the time his spoon rattled into the empty bowl of ice cream next to his cake plate. Cat's mom put both hands on the table. "Well, this has been such a wonderful evening, and you really made Cat's birthday unforgettable, James."

The two grown-ups looked at each other in a funny way. Cat's mom blushed. Then Yager wiped his mouth and stood, leaving the napkin on the table in front of him. "Let's not wait until she turns thirteen before we do it again."

Cat's mom tilted her head and smiled.

Jalen saw light at the end of the tunnel. He was going to make it, a clean getaway. Yager was going to let the whole thing drop, probably because he was more interested in Cat's mom than sending some twelve-year-old to a detention center for pinching a couple of baseballs he was going to give away in the first place.

"I'd like to ask a favor of you, though."

Jalen looked up and blinked. It was Yager speaking.

"Of course." Cat's mom blushed even harder.

"Well . . ." Yager looked at Jalen, and Jalen's stomach knotted up. "I'd like you to let me take Jalen home.

"I'd like to meet his father."

21

THANK-YOUS WERE DELIVERED ALL AROUND, AND
they migrated to the back of the house, where Yager had
tucked his black Lamborghini away.

Cat gave Jalen's hand a squeeze and offered him a sad
look. "Tell your dad thanks for the cannoli."

Cat's mom gave the player's hand a similar squeeze
and said something to him that Jalen couldn't hear.
Daniel walked alongside Jalen all the way to the car,
then whispered softly, "At least you get to ride in a
Lamborghini."

"Yeah, to my execution." Jalen didn't even look at his
friend; he was too worried about losing his dinner.

With a strong electric hum, the car doors opened the

way a ladybug opens its wings before flight, forward and up. The inside looked like a spaceship.

"Go ahead," Yager said. "Get in."

Jalen slipped into the palm of the leather seat and put his seat belt on. Yager did the same. The doors hummed shut. Jalen's friends stared with a mixture of envy and dread as the car rumbled to life. They backed up slowly and then crept around the corner of the mansion, but once they were out of sight, Yager stepped on the gas, and they zipped down the long, curving drive like it was a ride on the midway at the Westchester County Fair.

They were halfway down Old Post Road when the phone rang.

Yager pressed a button on the steering wheel. "Hello?"

"James?"

Yager's face fell instantly. "Hello, Jeffrey . . . I didn't know you had this number."

"Joe gave it to me." The Yankees GM sounded uptight. "Uh . . . we need to talk."

22

YAGER TIGHTENED HIS GRIP ON THE WHEEL AND pulled over. He ignored Jalen and leaned toward the glowing lights and dials of the dashboard, his face lit by their green radiance. "About what?"

"Cunningham's doing great in Toronto. He'll be playing second base against Chicago, and we'll see if he sticks." The GM's words filled the car like a layer of frost.

Jalen knew what it meant. It was the beginning of the end. Charlie Cunningham was an up-and-comer, a beefy young infielder, light on his feet but heavy in the hitting department. It seemed impossible, but Jalen knew these things happened, even to the great ones like Yager. Jalen's already twisted insides knotted up even tighter.

He guessed from the sight of Yager's gritted teeth that the Yankee star felt the same way he did, maybe worse.

Yes, definitely worse.

And in that moment, Jalen's sense of self-preservation—that instinct he felt certain came straight from his missing mom—asked the obvious question: Would Yager be so upset Jalen could escape the horror of having his father find out about the stolen balls? It was possible, and, as bad as Jalen felt for his hero, he couldn't help his own mental dash for daylight. He listened now with care and interest, because the next few moments might hold the key to his freedom.

Yager sat silent, but finally spoke. "You can't do this."

"Yeah. I can." Jeffrey Foxx's voice sounded suddenly light and cheery. "Your contract is up at the end of this season anyway. Look at your numbers, James. Also, there's your ankle."

"The ankle is fine." Yager rotated his foot. "The hydrotherapy is great, and the trainer says I'll be fine to play by Tuesday. My numbers are gonna bounce. It's only a slump, Jeffrey. I've got good years in me—you *know* that."

A car zipped past them going the other way. Yager's face was briefly lit up by the headlights, and his expression made Jalen think of a horror movie.

The GM cleared his throat on the other end of the call. "Your batting average these past three weeks is under a hundred and trending negative. It's a sinking ship, James. It happens to everyone. Look at Derek."

"Derek went out on *top*, Jeffrey!" Yager snarled. "I think I deserve the same courtesy."

"This phone call was a courtesy, James. I'm easing you out because I'm a nice guy. I'm sorry you don't see it that way." The GM's voice turned bitter. "You've got the next week to give the home crowd plenty of waves and smiles. We don't need Cunningham to beat the White Sox."

"And if I climb out of this?" Yager's voice had the edge of desperation. "What if I bat a thousand Wednesday? Then again on Thursday and Friday? Then it's not a sinking ship, is it?"

"Who doesn't love a comeback?" The GM sounded like a barber handing out a lollipop to some kid. "This isn't personal, James. This is about the New York Yankees winning a pennant, putting the best players on the field. Numbers don't lie. You bat a thousand in these next three games, and I'll extend that contract."

Yager's face was so screwed up, Jalen thought he might be ready to scream, but instead he nodded violently. "Okay. Numbers. You got it, Jeffrey. I'll give you your numbers."

"Right, but if you don't, we're square, right?" the GM said. "No drama, right, James? Just a nice press conference, thanking the club."

"You mean thanking the GM?"

"It's not about me. It's a team thing. Hey, got a call coming in from Mattingly on that Suarez trade. Good luck Wednesday." The phone went dead.

Yager sat for a full minute, just gripping the wheel.

Finally he sighed and looked over at Jalen, shaking his head. "Bad night for us both, I guess."

Jalen's mouth fell open. He couldn't believe Yager was still going to ruin Jalen's life when his own career was about to crash and burn. Did the man have no pity?

Yager put the car back into gear and checked his mirror before pulling back out onto the road. A car was coming, so Yager paused. A million things skittered through Jalen's mind. He knew he'd have one chance and only one chance to alter the collision course his life was on—as well as help Yager. He needed to speak before they moved. The moment would be over. His last chance would be blown.

The car zipped past, and before Yager could pull away, Jalen spoke.

"I can help you."

23

YAGER KEPT HIS FOOT ON THE BRAKE AND LOOKED

over at Jalen. "That's not even funny, kid."

Jalen nodded. "I can, though. I can help."

Yager snorted. "Right, kid. You and a truckload of rab-bits' feet."

"It's got nothing to do with luck," Jalen said, knowing that he had to keep talking, had to keep Yager's foot on that brake. He took a deep breath and talked fast. "I can tell you what the next pitch is going to be. I don't know how I know, but I *know*. You can ask my friends. I do it all the time when we're watching a game. I can do it better when I'm there, like my own games, or once when my dad took me to Yankee Stadium for my birthday. Then I'm almost a hundred percent. I'm telling you. I can *show* you."

Yager's face darkened. He glared at Jalen. "Kid, this is a bad moment for me. Don't make it worse. You're a thief, now you're a liar? This won't make things better."

Jalen's eye began to fill with tears. Desperation burned inside him. "I'm not lying! Ask Cat. Call her. Ask her. Cat doesn't lie. She'll tell you. I can *show* you. Saturday Night Baseball. It's on right now. The Royals and the Mariners. I'm telling you, I *know* what the next pitch is going to be, not a hundred percent, but ninety-five, easy. Isn't that all you'd need to go four-for-four, Mr. Yager? If you know the pitch coming at you? If you don't have to react to what you see? You know it's a curve, or a fastball down the middle, or a slider coming at you? You can adjust *before* the pitch, and when it comes, you're just waiting for it and . . . *pow!*

"Please! Just ask Cat. Let me show you. How can it hurt to just see? If I can't do it, you can take me to my dad *and* the police, but don't do this without letting me show you. It could mean everything, not just to me, but to *you*."

Yager stared at Jalen hard. The scowl was still in place, but he was chewing on his bottom lip.

Jalen closed his eyes and said a prayer.

24

WITHOUT A WORD, YAGER SLIPPED THE CAR OUT
of gear and picked up his phone. He hit a number and it
began to ring over the speaker system.

"Hello?"

Jalen's heart soared at the sound of Cat's mom.

"Victoria? It's James." Yager spoke into the windshield,
like there was someone on the other side of the glass. "I
know this sounds strange, but could I ask Cat a quick question? Her friend and I have a . . . a little bet going here. . . ."

"Oh. Of course. Again, I so appreciate your coming to dinner, and I know Gary does too, especially since he couldn't
be here. Cat's still on cloud nine. Hang on, James. . . ."

They could hear Cat's mom talking to her in a muffled
voice before she got on the phone.

"Hello? Jalen?"

"It's me and Jalen," Yager said. "In my car. Cat, this is silly, I know, but Jalen is insisting that he can predict the next pitch in a ball game, and I know that's not possible, but he says you think so too. I know it's fun to joke around, but you don't really believe that, right?"

Cat went silent. Jalen thought he could hear her breathing.

"Cat? I'm sorry. This is silly stuff. We're just goofing around here." Yager sounded apologetic but pleased. "I'll let you go. Happy birthday, Cat."

Yager looked at his phone and his thumb wavered over the screen, ready to disconnect.

"Wait!" It was Cat. "He can do it, Mr. Yager. Jalen *can* predict the next pitch. I know it sounds crazy, and we don't even know how, but he *can*. I think it's numbers or percentages or something. He's a wonk in math. Maybe it's body language too. I have no idea, but it's like this gift. It's magic. He does it in his own Little League games, and he does it if we watch a game on TV, too."

"Okay, Cat." Yager's voice got low and soft. "Thank you. I appreciate your thoughts. Good night."

Yager hung up and turned to Jalen. "You know I still don't believe you."

Jalen blinked and nodded. "You don't have to. Just let me show you."

Yager nodded and put the car back into gear. He checked the road for traffic, then spun the car around and punched the accelerator. They whizzed back up Old Post Road, past Mount Tipton, and turned into the gates where Yager's brick mansion rose up in front of them like a fortress.

They pulled into the circle and got out. The bronze angels splashed and struggled, frozen forever with their prize trumpet just out of reach.

Yager turned and flashed a scowl back at Jalen as he walked. "You know, I can't believe I'm doing this."

Jalen climbed the steps behind the famous Yankees player and followed him inside.

25

JALEN TOOK A DEEP BREATH.

A massive chandelier hung above him, its crystals sparkling with the hint of a million tiny rainbows. The tall marble columns, huge oil paintings, and alcoves where bronze sculptures were tucked away like treasures all fell to the back of Jalen's mind. It was the chandelier he couldn't stop staring at.

"Come on, kid." Yager sounded impatient, like he wanted to dispose of this nonsense.

Jalen forced his feet to move across the giant oriental rug, deep blue and thick as a close-cut grass lawn, and down a long hallway. Yager disappeared into a doorway without looking back. Jalen followed him down some stairs before entering a cave of dark wood. A bar stood at one end and a wall-size screen at the other. A plush couch faced the screen and a large fireplace was beneath the screen, cold and empty. The couch filled the middle of the room along with plump leather chairs surrounding a low round table. The walls held a dozen or so large framed photos, portraits of Yager with other famous people: President Obama, Peyton Manning, Jeter, DiCaprio, Denzel, Shaq, and others he knew but whose names didn't spring to mind. Each was set in a wood panel and lit by a small brass light.

Yager ignored the photos, picked up the remote, and plunked himself down on the couch.

"Sit," he said.

Jalen sat at the other end while his host brought Saturday Night Baseball up on the screen. Edinson Vólquez was on the mound, winding up.

"What's it gonna be?" Yager blurted out the question.

"Uh . . ."

The pitch smacked the catcher's mitt. A fastball down the middle.

"Too late," Yager said.

"I can't do it that fast." Jalen felt his insides squirm. Even the eyes of the famous people's photos around the room seemed to accuse him of lying.

"How fast can you do it?" Yager was slumped into the

couch with the remote in his hand, staring at the screen, which lit his bored, angry face in an eerie light.

"I need the count. I need the inning. The batter. I need to see the game," Jalen said.

"Okay, see it." Yager hit the mute button and the announcers went quiet.

"I'd like to hear it if I can too, please." Jalen clutched his hands together. Vólquez was already winding up again.

"What's the pitch? What's the pitch?" Yager insisted in a bitter tone.

"Uh . . ."

The batter swung and missed, striking out, and banged his bat in the dirt as he walked away.

"Can't do it, can you?" Yager jumped up out of his seat, glaring down on Jalen. "Okay, joke's up, kid. Let's see what your dad thinks about all this."

"No! Wait!" Jalen pleaded, fighting back tears. "Give me a chance. Why won't you give me a chance? Why are you so *angry*?"

"Angry?" Yager seemed to consider the word, chewing on his lip while he gazed at Jalen. Finally he sighed. "You're right. I am angry. I hate Jeffrey Foxx. He thinks he knows baseball, but he doesn't. It's *not* just about numbers. I can . . ."

The player sat down and turned on the sound. "Okay,

kid. Show me. Let's see if you really can do something. Anything would help me at this point, so I should at least let you show me so I can say I did everything possible when I'm sitting on a beach chair a month from now in Tahiti."

Jalen sighed and returned his attention to the screen. Vólquez was in his windup again and threw a curveball that went way wide of the plate for a ball. Jalen forced himself to study the screen. Third inning. Mariners up 1–0. A man on first. Two outs. Kyle Seager was the batter, a slugging infielder with an average strikeout rate and a high line-drive rate. His home run production had gone up for five years in a row. Jalen wished he'd seen the first two innings, but as he opened his mouth to explain how he usually needed time to see the pattern, Vólquez nodded to the catcher and checked the runner at first.

"Changeup." The name of the pitch popped out of Jalen's mouth.

Vólquez wound up and threw an eighty-three-mile-an-hour changeup. Seager swung and missed, making it a 1–1 count.

"Hey, you're right." Yager glanced at Jalen and sat up. "But you've got a one-in-four chance, right? Vólquez only throws four pitches, right?"

"Right." Jalen nodded but kept his eyes on the game. The camera cut around the stadium, showing pictures of fans, the stadium lights, the managers, setting the scene. Jalen gritted his teeth because he wanted to see the pitcher.

"Yeah," Yager said, "so, good guess."

The screen cut quickly to Vólquez.

"Fastball!" Jalen blurted. "Four-seam."

Vólquez threw a four-seam fastball high and outside for a second ball.

"Kid, if you can only pick it when he's already in his windup, how is that supposed to help me?" Yager asked, sounding more sad now than angry.

"I gotta see the pitcher. I gotta see it all. It's better in person, and I have to see the pitcher before he gets into his windup. I can tell before he winds up, but not like this. Wait. I'll show you. I got the changeup right, didn't I? And the fastball? Give me a chance."

Yager sat back into the couch and folded his arms across his chest.

This time the camera stayed on the pitcher, and before he went into his windup, Vólquez shook the catcher off.

"Another four-seam fastball," said Jalen.

That's what it was. Seager swung and missed.

"Two-two count," Yager said.

"Here comes the sinker," Jalen said without thinking.

"You know that? Already?" Yager stared at him, hard.

Jalen nodded because he *knew*.

Vólquez nodded to his catcher and went into his windup. Jalen knew this was the tipping point. If the pitcher threw a sinker, Yager would believe.

If not . . .

Jalen was going home.

26

SEAGER SWUNG FOR THE FENCES AND MISSED.

The ump jagged his thumb and barked.

Jalen sat silently as the announcers showed the replay from behind the pitcher and traced the path of the pitch, a rope that dropped off the table at the last instant, a nasty sinker. Vólquez pumped his fist. The inning ended, and the TV went to a shaving cream commercial.

Yager turned to Jalen, still frowning. "I want to see more."

Jalen nodded, let out a breath, and sat back into the soft leather cushions. They could watch as much as the Yankees star liked.

"You want something to drink?" Yager asked, getting up and heading for the bar.

Jalen smiled but tried not to let it get out of control, even though he knew his entire life had just taken a turn for the better. "I'll take a Pepsi if you have it."

27

IT WASN'T EASY TO CONVINCE THE YANKEES STAR.

If Jalen hadn't known his dad would be at the diner until well after midnight, he would have had to call home and try to explain what was going on.

Yager couldn't get enough. Even as the game ended in the bottom of the ninth after Jalen called the last pitch—a changeup knocked out of the park with two runners on base—Yager wanted more and kept flipping through channels.

"That's the last game." Jalen pointed at the clock. "And I should get home."

The Yankees player looked at the clock with alarm. "Holy crow. What are your parents going to say?"

"My . . . I only have a dad."

"Oh. Divorce? My parents got divorced when I was ten. I know it hurts." Yager frowned.

"I don't even know if they're divorced," Jalen said. "We don't really talk about it. She was a singer, I know that. I think she had some big chance or something, but still, you just leave your family?"

Yager nodded with understanding. "My dad took off too. Him and his secretary. Moved to Australia. But you can either let things like that ruin you or spur you on to do great things."

Jalen was confused and didn't hide it.

"My parents' divorce probably helped me make it to the pros," Yager explained. "I felt like the whole thing was my fault, and I wanted to be worthy of something. So I set out to prove it with baseball. I mean, I had talent, too, but work? I'd get in the batting cage and hit until my hands bled. I'm serious."

Jalen nodded. "I get that. I want to do that too, make it to the pros, and I'm going to work hard. That you better believe."

"Is your dad going to let you help me here?" Yager obviously wanted to get back on solid ground. "Will he be okay with all this?"

"What do you mean?"

"So, I need you at Yankee Stadium. We need some signals." Yager stared into empty space for a moment. "And I've got to get you some seats. Your dad can come with you."

Jalen shook his head. "You play the next three games at night. My dad can't. He works."

"Maybe Victoria and Cat could bring you?" Yager looked at Jalen for the answer.

Jalen could only shrug. "I don't know. Maybe."

"Would your dad let you?"

"If you asked, he would." Jalen opened his mouth to say something else, then stopped.

"What?" Yager narrowed his eyes.

Jalen had an idea. It was a bit bold, brazen maybe, brash? Something Cat would do. Oh, Cat would definitely do it. Jalen could hear her now, in his mind.

Do it, Jalen! Just do it!

28

"I DON'T WANT TO MAKE IT LIKE YOU *HAVE* TO DO
this." Jalen tried to sound as casual as he could, even though
he was brimming with excitement. "It's just that . . ."

"What, kid? Some autographs or something? Spit it out."

Jalen took a breath and spoke fast. "Well, I didn't have
enough money for my travel team, and my coach said my
dad could make some sandwiches instead, but he works
like a dog as it is, and I was thinking you could maybe
have your foundation give me that money. I mean, no big
deal, right?"

Yager frowned. "I'm cutting you a break by not turning you in for stealing baseballs and now you want more
from me?"

"I was just doing what your own foundation is supposed to be doing." Jalen felt suddenly angry and frustrated, and he just cut loose. "But I'm sure you have no idea, right? It's like your social media. Someone does it for you, right? Well, I had the chance to play summer ball but I needed some money for the fees, exactly what your foundation *says* it wants to do, but what you get if you're a kid who really needs money for baseball is answering machines and form replies."

Yager stared hard.

Jalen calmed himself and softened his voice. "Is it really that big a deal? It's the last thing my dad needs, to make a bunch of free sandwiches and then a banquet for the team. That's not going to help him get out of the hole he's been in since forever."

Yager chewed his lip again, then pointed the remote at Jalen like he was changing a channel. "You help me go four-for-four on Wednesday, and I'll get the foundation to pay it."

"All four hundred ninety dollars?"

Yager smiled and nodded. "Sure. No problem."

Jalen beamed. "Then let's go meet my dad."

29

JALEN BURST WITH PRIDE AS HE CLIMBED OUT OF
JY's Lamborghini, but no one was there to notice. Inside
the diner, five loud, sloppy college kids sat in the corner
booth by the counter. On the other side, in the dining room,
were two couples, one young and eating bread, the other
middle-aged and whispering to each other over glasses of
wine and fried calamari.

Greta, his father's frumpiest waitress, with short, dyed-
black hair, burst from the kitchen and hustled by with a
tray of burgers, cursing under her breath at the college
kids. She didn't even notice Yager. No one did.

"Come on." Jalen led the player back into the kitchen.
His father was sweating over a hissing stove.

"Jalen!" He glanced up only for a moment. "Hand me the parmesan. The parmesan! Jalen!"

Jalen did as he was told and stood there with Yager while his father rasped dusty flakes from the wooden block of cheese. Finally he tilted his head, added another sprinkle, and then eased a fine chop out of the pan and onto a bed of arugula on one of his best plates. He turned quickly to the oven, brushing past Yager and removing a pan of eggplant rollatini tucked beneath a blanket of mozzarella. He added that to another plate, then dribbled red sauce from a pot, before depositing a pinch of basil and salt.

"Greta!" Jalen's father bellowed as the waitress banged in through the swinging doors with a pink mess all over the front of her apron.

She held her hands in the air and wore a look of raging disgust. "Rich brats! One puked on me! Puked! All over!"

She made a beeline for the sink, flung her apron in a corner, and began scrubbing her arms and face in a torrent of water.

"Jimmy, get the mop! Go clean it!" Jalen's dad yelled at a stringy young man with tattoos covering his arms, who was busy loading the dishwasher. "And put on your hat!"

Jimmy slapped a white paper hat on his head, grabbed the mop, and headed out into the war zone.

"Jalen, you have to take this out for me. I can't go out

like this, and I've got rice balls to do and table three's been waiting too long already." Without pause, Jalen's dad handed him the two dinner plates. "Table seven."

Jalen gave James Yager an embarrassed look.

"Help your dad." Yager spoke in a low voice.

"I'm sorry." Jalen's dad gave Yager a glance as he got back to his stove. "I'll talk to you in a minute."

"He doesn't mean to be rude," Jalen said. "He's just working."

"Take the food." Yager nodded toward the dining room. "I'm fine."

Jalen backed out through the swinging doors. He ignored the college kids laughing uproariously in the corner and delivered the food to table seven with as much dignity as he could muster. The serious middle-aged couple were blinking at the booth with the students now, not happy.

"Can I offer you some fresh ground pepper?" Jalen tried to place himself in their sight line to block their view of the corner booth. One of the kids let out an outrageous fart, and they all laughed hysterically.

The man looked around Jalen before asking him, "Can someone please get them to quiet down?"

"Uh, yes," Jalen said, wondering what they thought a twelve-year-old kid was going to do. *"Buon appetito."*

He retreated to the kitchen, where Greta was now crying and his father was putting out a small fire on the stove.
Jalen wanted to cry himself when he saw another burning
welt on his father's forearm.

"Dad, seven wants someone to get those college kids to
be quiet."

His father placed the fried rice balls onto a small plate,
doused them in red sauce, and added his pinches of basil,
salt, and this time pepper before he looked up. "Greta, you
cannot cry. You gotta take this to table three, and I gotta
get those boys to stop-a the noise. I got a stuffed calamari
in the oven."

His father flipped off his apron, mopped his brow, and
looked up at Yager. "I think I see you before. In a shaving
commercial. For the razors, no?"

"That'd be me." Yager rubbed his chin. "Maybe I can
help with the kids in the corner. You keep cooking."

Jalen's father's eyes twinkled with delight. "Jalen, did
you bring me an angel from above?"

His father turned back toward the stove, and Jalen
followed Yager out into the dining room, burning with
embarrassment. He'd so wanted Yager to be impressed,
because in the back of his mind—as long as he could
remember—he'd dared to dream the ballplayer might
have dinner there himself some night. Yager stopped

at the table and looked down at the college kids with a smile.

"Hey," one of the kids said through a mouthful of cheeseburger, "JY!"

They all stopped eating.

Another one of them burped. "Naw, he *looks* like James Yager. JY wouldn't be in this dump." The kid slurped at his shake.

"Yeah, I am James Yager," the ballplayer said patiently. "I'm headed out, but if you guys want to do some selfies, we can—only outside, because see that woman over there?"

"With the fat guy?" one kid slurred.

"Yeah, that's my sister and her husband. It's their anniversary, so . . . you guys are a little . . . uh, you're wrecking the mood of the whole thing."

"We're wreckers," a redheaded kid chirped with a happy nod. "But I'm up for a selfie with JY. Can we bring our burgers?"

"Sure." Yager nodded. "Let's just keep it down, though, okay?"

The whole crew got up, whispering loudly and barely suppressing their giggles at the sight of Jimmy with his mop, but leaving a pile of twenty-dollar bills on the table. Outside in the chilly air, JY stood beside each one of them, forcing smiles in the explosion of flashes as they snapped away, taking pictures until Yager held up both hands. "Okay, guys. Gotta go. You too. Time now."

"Aww," they all said.

"Yup, it's time. No, not back inside. That would defeat the purpose."

"Like you defeated the Angels in the ALCS!"

"Exactly."

"You know, you're my hero. No lies."

"Wonderful. I appreciate that. Call a cab and head on home, okay? Good night, guys." Yager turned without looking back and steered Jalen back inside, stopping at the door to make sure none of them followed.

"Thanks." Jalen felt a mixture of shame and gratefulness.

"You just do your thing with me on Wednesday. That's all the thanks I need. Come on, let's talk to your dad."

Greta passed them on their way into the kitchen, composed, but with streaks of eye makeup on her face giving her a haunted look as she delivered the appetizers to table three. Jalen's dad finally slowed down. Table three was having pasta for their dinner, and it required little work, so already his father had begun to scrape the surface of the stove, cleaning it for the night.

"Dad, this is James Yager," Jalen said.

Jalen's dad stopped to firmly shake Yager's hand. "I know,

I know. The shaving man from the TV. He's famous, no?"

"He's famous for playing baseball, Dad. The Yankees?"

"Ahh. The only famous athletes I know about, they are the football players. You know Ronaldo?"

"That's soccer, Dad."

"Yes, of course. Soccer. Mr. Yager, *grazie*. If I can do anything for you, you just tell me." Jalen's dad had his hands on his hips, and he wore an earnest smile.

"That's music to my ears, Mr. DeLuca."

"Please, Fabio to you."

"Great. So, Fabio, how can I say this?" The famous baseball player wore a nervous smile. "I'd actually like to borrow your son."

Jalen's dad suddenly scowled, and he shook his head violently. "No, Mr. Yager. That I cannot let you do."

30

THE NEXT DAY JALEN AND HIS TWO FRIENDS SAT
on bales of hay in the hideaway they'd made in the loft of
the barn. It smelled like horses. Jalen was telling them the
story of what had happened at the diner the night before.

"But he's letting you, right?" Daniel gripped Jalen's
arm when he heard the part about Jalen's dad saying no
to Yager borrowing him. "Your dad?"

Jalen laughed. "Yes, he's letting me. My dad thought he
wanted to adopt me or something. I don't know. You know
my dad."

Cat laughed too. "Did your dad *really* think when he
came here from Italy that he was going to California, but
ended up in Florida?"

"Couldn't speak a word of English." Jalen shook his head and sighed, because he'd told the story before. "The travel agent in this little seaside Italian town where he grew up took all his money and booked a ticket that would get him to Hollywood. Turns out there's a Hollywood in Florida, though. Didn't have a dime when he got there and figured it out. Hitchhiked to relatives in New York and found a job spinning pizzas in Bronxville. It's funnier when he tells it, though."

"Yeah, I bet." Daniel shook his head. "This is really unbelievable, right? And you're going to Yankee Stadium later today to see everything? The locker room? The players' lounge? I mean, everything?"

"He wants to do a dry run when no one's around," Jalen said. "I guess he got some tickets lined up from the owner for Wednesday night. He said they're right behind the on-deck circle."

Daniel stood up and waved his arms. "I mean, this is all really happening, it's James Yager . . ."

"Thanks to Cat." Jalen looked her in the eyes until she blushed.

"I think it just all worked out, right? Who knew my mom was even friends with him?" Cat said.

"Do you think she *likes* him?" Daniel raised an eyebrow.

Cat frowned. "I don't know. She's my mother, but she's

been married a couple times before, and I never got what she saw in Gary."

"You never saw someone wanting to live in Mount Tipton?" Daniel's eyes widened. "Seriously?"

"My dad was a teacher and her last husband was a plumber. She's not about that, I'm telling you both. Anyway, don't talk like that about my mom." Cat's eyes blazed.

"Okay," Daniel muttered.

"I didn't even say anything," Jalen complained.

Cat calmed down and said, "I like James Yager, though."

Jalen picked a stalk of hay from a bale and bit on the end so its bristle tip swayed in front of his face like a pesky fly. "How many famous guys would've helped my dad like that last night?"

"Well, you are about to save his career." Cat paused, then asked, "Why the face?"

Jalen removed the stem of hay. "Well, saving his career doesn't do me any good at all if I can't save my own."

"What do you mean?" Daniel asked.

"We start Rockets practice tomorrow night, right?" Jalen asked.

"Yeah."

"What's the schedule after that?"

Daniel shrugged. "I'm sure we'll get it tomorrow."

"Right, but it's going to include some other practice

days this week, right?" Jalen bent the hay stem. "We've got a tournament this weekend, right?"

"Sure, in White Plains."

"So, Yager wants me at the stadium Wednesday, Thursday, and Friday. I don't see how I can do that without missing a practice, and I heard Coach Gamble doesn't like it when you miss practice. I heard Mark Scofield missed a practice for Little League because he had to go to his brother's wedding in Nashville, but that wasn't a good enough excuse for Coach Gamble and he didn't let Mark play for two games."

"Yeah, but this is for James *Yager*," Cat said. "Even Gamble has to see that."

"When it comes to the Gambles," Jalen said, "I think you throw the rule book out the window."

31

LATER THAT SAME DAY, YAGER'S LAMBORGHINI
flew down the highway, passing cars like they were parked.

"You always drive this fast?" Jalen felt surprisingly relaxed, like, how could James Yager ever get into a crash? Something told Jalen he couldn't.

"Pretty much." Yager switched the radio to WFAN, a sports talk station.

"*. . . that and a dollar will get you a cup of coffee.*"

"*A dollar? You can't get a coffee for a buck anymore, just like the Sox can't get a relief pitcher who can hold a lead.*"

"*Okay, a cup of hot water, for tea. And speaking of hot water, not for tea, but real hot water, let's switch over to the Yankees' one-time star second baseman, James Yager.*"

Jalen's and Yager's eyes met briefly.

"*Hot water, indeed. Word on the street is Cunningham gets the start against Chicago. Now, JY does have the ankle thing.*"

"*He's had the ankle thing since last season.*"

"*But our sources tell us it's more than the ankle, it's the batting average that's starting to look like my math average in high school.*"

"*You passed math?*"

"*Barely, and that's where JY's average is headed, so why not put him out of his misery?*"

"*Like an old dog? You'd do that? To James Yager? The James Yager? Have you no heart?*"

"*What heart I have—and it's not very big—belongs to the Bronx Bombers. Great ones come and great ones go. Cunningham's on the rise. Numbers don't lie.*"

"*I know one guy in the Yankees front office who's so good at numbers, he probably knows what size underwear you've got on.*"

"*Jeffrey Foxx would be offended by that comment. I think you should—*"

Yager flipped the radio off. "Idiots."

"My dad says they don't talk like that in Italy about their sports teams. He says they respect their players." Jalen hoped he was being helpful.

"I'd head right over there—to Italy—if they had a base-ball league. I can't stand these mush brains."

Jalen nodded, and they rode in silence through the Bronx until they turned a corner, and there was Yankee Stadium, rising up from its surroundings like a cathedral.

"Awesome." Jalen held his breath as they turned into the tunnel leading beneath the magnificent structure.

A guard saw Yager, smiled, opened the gate, and waved them on in. At first Jalen was confused because it was just like any other parking garage, maybe just a bit cleaner with white-painted walls, but the same cinder block and concrete you'd see in any garage. They got out, and his excitement began to fizzle at the plain blue metal door. They entered a bland stairwell and climbed up a level before Yager reached for the handle of another metal door that had a Yankees logo on it.

When he opened that door, though, Jalen followed him down a short hallway, and it was like a thou-sand Christmas mornings and birthday parties rolled into one moment. It was the players' lounge. Leather couches and flat-screen TVs, small round tables, drink machines, a snack bar, lush carpet, and mood lighting. Photos of old Yankees covered the walls. It felt rich . . . it felt famous . . . and Jalen was beside *the* James Yager, who walked right on through and into the locker room like it was no big deal. In the locker room, Jalen's feet froze on the thick blue carpet.

He had to stop and look around at the wide spaces carved into the walls and filled with all kinds of shoes and shirts and gloves and hats and anything you could imagine needing to wear on the diamond. Each had its own fancy leather swivel chair, and many of the players had photos of loved ones taped to the flat surfaces surrounding their personal mirrors. Above each space, he saw the names: Sabathia, Hutt, Tanaka, Tollerson, Joe Ros, and Gardner. All there.

"I mean . . ." Jalen still couldn't move. "Wow."

Yager grabbed a bat from his locker and looked back at him. "Come on. Out on the field."

Jalen followed him out the door, cutting through a concrete tunnel, then up some rubber-padded steps into the dugout.

"Wow." Jalen couldn't help it. It was just what came out.

Yager kept going, up the steps and out onto the grass. "I want to do a dry run to make sure we can see each other when I'm batting. Here's where you'll be."

Just over a low concrete wall, dark-blue seats with thick padding began the first row.

"Me? Here?"

"Sure," Yager said. "Let me help you over."

It wasn't hard, and in seconds Jalen was standing on the other side of the wall. Yager pointed with his bat to the third seat in from the dugout. "Try that. Sit."

Snuggling into the cushioned seat, Jalen watched the Yankees player walk out to home plate and circle it so he stood the way he would if he were facing a pitcher— the way he *would* be standing when he faced the White Sox pitcher Wednesday. Jalen looked up and around at the pennants snapping in the wind. Layer after layer of sweeping sections of empty seats jutted out and rose up toward the sky. His eyes traveled over the open end of the stadium, where scoreboards and billboards sprang up from behind the wall, blotting out the neighborhood beyond. If Jalen sat in this seat Wednesday, he'd be closer to the action than the players in the dugout. Jalen had never even known such a seat existed. On TV it didn't look that close, and the one time his father had taken him to Yankee Stadium, they'd been so far away that the players on the field looked like punctuation marks.

Out on the field JY got into his stance, glanced at Jalen, looked at the mound, stepped out of the box, and looked at Jalen again before shouting, "That's the seat!"

Yager was marching toward him with a grin.

"Who sits here usually?" Jalen asked Yager, who now stood with his hand on the low concrete wall. Jalen was trying to imagine the kind of a life you'd have to lead to be able to watch a Yankees game from this spot.

"Well, like I said, these are the owner's seats, but he doesn't sit here. Probably friends or business associates or big sponsors. You can see the pitcher well from here, right?" Yager asked.

"Perfectly."

"Good." Yager tapped the padding on the outside of the concrete wall with his bat. "Tell you what. You can wait here or in the locker room. I'm going upstairs to see if Mr. Brenneck is around and make sure he's got these seats specifically set aside. We can't afford for you not to be in this first row. You want to stay right here?"

"Here is fine." Jalen sat back down and took a deep breath, imagining what it might be like Wednesday during the game, hoping the thrill of it wouldn't interfere with his ability to predict pitches. He felt light-headed with excitement.

Aloud he said, "I'm in Yankee Stadium, right on the *field*."

Yager was gone for maybe ten minutes before Jalen grew restless. There wasn't a soul around. He had Yankee Stadium to himself and he was struck by a brilliant idea. Remembering the brief discussion his friends had on the train back from selling Yager's baseballs, Jalen hopped over the wall and crouched in the dirt. Using his house key, he dug a little hole and scooped up the dirt in his palm before standing and depositing it in his pocket.

He looked around. No bells or alarms went off. He didn't hear or see a thing except a handful of seagulls wheeling beyond the scoreboard. Jalen knew both Daniel and Cat would love a bit of the Yankees infield, so he crouched down again and dug a slightly bigger hole, scooping a much bigger handful of dirt.

Jalen was focused on his pocket and getting all the dirt in there without making a total mess of his pants when he heard footsteps below him from the dugout. Before he could move, a sharp-faced man appeared and briskly climbed the stairs. Jalen felt the hair on his neck stand. He recognized Jeffrey Foxx from his picture, but the GM's eyes were so pale they looked like bullet holes surrounded by perfect black circles, and they frightened Jalen even before he spoke. The GM's blond hair was cut close. He wore a dark-gray pinstripe suit with a bright-yellow bow tie, round gold glasses, and a bitter scowl. He was tan and tall, and somehow made Jalen think of a tennis player.

Jalen felt sick and certain he was somehow in the wrong place at the wrong time. He stopped loading the dirt into his pocket, but froze and clenched what remained in his fist.

The GM looked at Jalen with disgust, and he wagged his head for someone behind him to hurry up. Two large city policemen marched up the stairs with hats pulled down tight and guns and handcuffs strapped to their hips.

Jeffrey Foxx pointed at Jalen with lips compressed by anger. "Arrest this kid."

32

THE POLICE HAD JALEN BY EITHER ARM.

"Drop the dirt." The GM pointed at Jalen's tight fist.

Jalen opened it, and a dusty stream dribbled to the ground.

The police practically lifted him up before marching him down the concrete steps and through the dugout. Instead of taking a left to go through the locker room, they steered him to the right, past a batting cage and a garage-like area with some stationary bikes and a treadmill.

The GM spoke to one of the policemen as they walked. "I look out my office window and I see him out there digging. You believe that?"

"You want us to take him to the station?" the policeman

asked as they took Jalen through a door and into a concrete hallway.

"It's trespassing, right?" Foxx glared at Jalen as they waited for an elevator. "We have to set an example. I have no idea how he got in, but I'm sure he's got some buddies ready to pull the same stunt. We need to make it hurt."

"Breaking and entering?" the other policeman suggested.

"That'd put him in juvie lockup for sure unless somebody's got a good lawyer," said his fellow officer with a chuckle.

Jalen was paralyzed. He knew he had to talk and talk fast, but like in a bad dream, his mouth wouldn't do what his brain was telling it to do. The elevator dinged and opened. They took a short ride up and stepped out into an enormous entryway where a long desk and a pair of security guards faced a statue of George Steinbrenner. Jalen couldn't help looking all around. Above the bank of elevators behind him was a twenty-foot-high picture of Babe Ruth wearing the huge shiny crown of a king.

Through the glass in front of him, he could see a police car rested outside on the curb, doors open and lights turning. The noise of the policemen's feet, clapping on the shiny floor as they steered him toward it, increased his panic.

"Wait!" Jalen resisted, trying to pull away. His shout

echoed through the cavernous space. The security guards stared. Steinbrenner's statue seemed to purse its lips. The Babe seemed to be frowning just for him.

"Please!" Jalen looked around desperately for a friendly face, landing on the least friendly face of all, the dead-eyed GM with the yellow bow tie. "I'm with James Yager. He brought me."

One of the policemen dropped his arm, but the other laughed gruffly. "Yeah, and I'm having dinner tonight with Jeter. Let's go, kid."

The policeman holding him gave a gentle tug.

"Wait." Foxx looked suddenly fascinated. "Yager? Who are *you*?"

The elevator door behind them rumbled open and JY dashed across the floor, pulling up just short of Jalen. He was huffing for breath. "Hey, Jeffrey. Guys. This is . . . Jalen . . . he's okay. He's just a kid who lives in my town. Long story, but he's okay. He's with me."

"You left a kid just sitting out there in the stadium?" Foxx wrinkled his brow. "Where were you?"

"I had to see Mr. Brenneck."

Foxx knit his blond eyebrows together and spoke through his teeth in a low growl. "I told you ownership is on board with what's happening, James. You shouldn't have done that."

Yager shook his head. "No, I was getting some tickets. For the game. Jalen and a friend or two. His dad is my nutritional consultant. I promised him and . . . well . . . how many times do you get to see someone go four-for-four?"

Foxx wasn't amused. "I can't have this kid in Yankee Stadium, James. Not Wednesday night. Not ever."

"What?" Yager was stunned. "Why not?"

Foxx spoke through his teeth again, but this time even slower. "Because we found him digging up the infield and stealing the dirt."

33

YAGER BLINKED AND SNUCK QUICK GLANCES AT
each of the policemen. "Wait. What? Jeffrey, you didn't
just say he stole *dirt*, did you?"

"That's exactly what he was doing." Foxx jutted out his
chin. "That dirt's worth money. People sell that dirt on
eBay. This is Yankee Stadium."

"I know. I've been playing for this team for ten years,
Jeffrey." Yager seemed to grow taller. "He's a kid. He
wanted a little dirt."

"When I was a kid, I wanted a little candy," the GM said.
"You think I stole it?"

"Well, he put it back, didn't he?" Yager threw up his
hands.

"Yes, but only because I made him, and that doesn't change that he stole it," Foxx said.

Yager bit his lip, then said, "He's my guest. I said he could have the dirt, Jeffrey, so it's *not* stealing. *And* he put it back."

Jalen's jaw went slack. He couldn't believe that Yager had just lied to protect him.

The two men stared each other down for a few tense moments before Yager appealed to the police. "Right, guys? Not stealing if you have permission and you put it back."

"Uh . . ." The policeman who had Jalen's arm in his grip let go. "Yeah, that'd be correct."

"Maybe we should let you fellas work this out in private," said the other cop.

"Mr. Foxx?" asked the first.

The GM held up a hand and made small brushing motions without speaking, and the police made their way toward the exit, where the squad car waited.

"Let's all just relax." Yager put a hand on Jalen's shoulder.

The GM glared, his face the color of the police light. "Three more games with you, James. That's all I've got. *Then* I'll relax."

"Unless I go four-for-four in the next three games."

Yager smiled and gave Jalen's shoulder a squeeze. "This kid is like a giant rabbit's foot, Jeffrey. You may have to put up with me for quite a while yet."

"We'll see about that." The GM spun and marched toward the doors immediately beside the security desk, where the guards gawked.

"What are you people looking at?" Foxx roared. "Get back to work!"

34

"C'MON, KID." YAGER TURNED, AND JALEN followed him to the elevator they'd come up on. They got off and passed a dark-blue wall signed in silver by what looked like all the famous Yankees who'd ever put on the pinstripes. Jalen hesitated, but Yager kept going, obviously upset. They passed the clubhouse entrance and took another door leading down some stairs into the garage.

They rode in silence until they hit the thruway, and Yager pounded a hand on the steering wheel. "That Foxx . . . dirt."

"I'm sorry," Jalen said.

"Forget it." Yager waved his hand dismissively.

Jalen was horrified by the small deposit of infield dirt still in his pants pocket, and he covered the very slight bulge instinctively. "Did you get the tickets?"

Yager brightened. "Those I got. For Wednesday anyway. Four. Mr. Brenneck's assistant is leaving them at the will call window."

"Four?" Jalen felt a surge of joy. "For who?"

"Well, I figured you need an adult, so that's Victoria. She's going to have to bring Cat, and then I figured I might as well ask for four. One for your other little buddy."

"Daniel?" Jalen could only imagine his friend's face when saw those seats.

"Yeah, the wise guy. The 'Do you feel old?' guy."

"He didn't mean it."

"Anyway, I thought it'd be better for you to have some cushion, right? Not jam you into the crowd. People on either side of you. This way, it's less likely for anyone to figure out what we're doing." Yager wove the Lamborghini through traffic as he spoke. "So, we gotta figure some signals."

Suddenly Yager looked over at Jalen. "I can't believe I'm doing this. How desperate am I?"

"It's not desperate," Jalen said. "It's smart. You're using every resource available."

"I'm getting coaching from a twelve-year-old kid."

Yager sighed and shook his head, but then they talked about the signals they'd use for the various pitches. By the time Jalen got dropped off in front of the Silver Liner, they had it down pretty good.

Jalen got out of the car but didn't close the door. "You want to come in? My dad could make us something."

"No thanks, kid. I gotta get back. Get ready for Wednesday. Hit some balls in the cage, unless someone stole them all." Yager gave Jalen a serious look, then cracked a smile. "If this works, I'll not only pay your travel team fee, kid, I'll give you every ball in that batting cage. *If* it works."

Jalen closed the door and the car rumbled off. A middle-aged couple was coming out of the diner, and the man stopped and stared at the car with his mouth open. "Was that James Yager?"

"Yeah," Jalen said, and he marched into the diner to help his dad, feeling incredibly proud and excited, but also scared because he wasn't sure if they could really pull it off.

35

THE NEXT DAY IN SCHOOL, DANIEL COULDN'T
stop grinning. He questioned Jalen every free minute
they had—in the hallways, the lunchroom, gym class,
everywhere—over and over about the exact location of
their seats and what it had been like inside the locker
room. It seemed to make up for the bragging they had
to endure from the A's players, who'd won the league
championship the night before.

Maybe most of all, Daniel was excited about the little
bottle of dirt Jalen had given to him, explaining that
it had come from the Yankees infield. Jalen had found
two small empty bottles in the Silver Liner recycle bin,
stripped their labels, and carefully added the dirt from

his pocket before making new labels with a Sharpie: YANKEE STADIUM INFIELD.

When he wasn't showing it to anyone who'd look, even Chris, Daniel kept his hand clasped around the bottle in his pocket nearly the entire day. He told Jalen, "It's like having a slice of Mount Olympus in your pocket. Like it can give you superpowers."

Cat remained pretty calm about the whole Yankees thing—not just the dirt, but going to the game and everything. When they were sitting in their hideaway after school, Jalen asked her why she wasn't excited.

"You mean you want me to be bouncing off the walls like him." Cat nodded at Daniel, who had his baseball mitt on and was mimicking the spectacular plays they'd be seeing the Yankees make in the field, providing commentary all the while.

"And JY snags a line drive. He zips it to first." Daniel leaped and made a throwing motion as he fell in a pile of loose hay before pumping his arms in the air so they stuck up out of the hay he was buried in. "Turn two!"

Jalen laughed. "No, but you don't even seem happy about it."

"I'm just thinking," she said, "about how this can help *you*."

"This?"

"You're a baseball genius, Jalen. You're practically giv-ing it away." Cat picked a piece of hay out of Jalen's hair. "I want you to get something out of it more than Yager giving you a pass for taking those baseballs and paying your registration fee from a foundation that's *supposed* to do that already. Even he sees that you just took a shortcut to what his foundation is supposed to be doing."

"You mean he should pay me more?" Jalen asked.

"Maybe." She shrugged. "We'll see. If it saves his career? Why wouldn't he? Maybe we have you sign a contract or something. But in the meantime, I think I know what else we need to ask him to do. . . ."

Cat jumped up off the bale of hay she'd been sitting on. "Come on. Let's go."

"Where?" Jalen stood.

"Next door. To Yager's."

"We're just walking up to the front door?"

"Why not? We're neighbors, and now we're friends and business associates." Cat grabbed Daniel's hand and hauled him onto his feet. "Come on. We're going over the wall. I want to surprise him."

36

UP AND OVER THEY WENT. CAT, DANIEL, AND JALEN
marched through the trees, crossed the creek, then walked
straight across the grass to the circular driveway, past the
fountain, and right up to the front door, where Cat rang
the bell. The sound of the Rottweilers' barking exploded
from within, and they could hear the dogs throwing themselves at the door. Jalen and Daniel shifted uncomfortably
on their feet, but Cat rang the bell again despite the dogs.
Then they heard a sharp command and some more noise
from inside before the door swung open.

"What?" Yager wore jeans and a scruffy black T-shirt.
He peered past them down the driveway toward his gates.
"How'd you get in?"

"Let's not get caught up on details," Cat said. "We have to talk. Can we come in?"

"Can I say no?" The dogs were sitting alert, with low growls leaking from their throats.

"Not really." Cat smiled, moving past him into the grand entryway, ignoring the dogs. "Should we sit down?"

"Should we?" Yager asked.

"Let's," said Cat.

JY gave a command, and the two dogs disappeared.

"Wow." Daniel's eyes were the size of saucers, and he had tucked himself behind Jalen. "Are they gone now?"

"Yeah. They won't hurt you," Yager said before he led them into a great room overlooking the pool and the lawn they'd crossed from Cat's place. "Sit."

They sat in a row on the thick-cushioned couch, with Daniel gawking at the paintings on the walls before he pointed at the bookshelves next to a huge, empty fireplace. "You read all those?"

Yager sat across from them in an enormous leather chair, and he looked over his shoulder and snorted. "No. They're for show. My decorator put them there."

"Decorator?" Daniel's eyebrows disappeared beneath his dark bangs. "Like a cake?"

"No, for the house," Yager said. "The furniture, paintings, everything. I don't know how to do it."

Daniel looked around and sighed in apparent disapproval. "There's no baseball stuff. I thought you'd have some pictures. Jalen said there were pictures."

Jalen felt his face flush. "That's . . . not why we're here."

"Why *are* you here?" Yager asked, looking at Cat.

"Quid pro quo," said Cat.

"Oh, really?" Yager scratched his chin.

"Squid?" Daniel leaned forward and stared at Cat.

"*Quid* pro quo," Cat explained to Daniel. "I do something for you, you do something for me."

She turned to the Yankees second baseman. "Jalen is saving your career."

"And I'm not pressing charges. *And* I'm paying the registration fee for that travel team. That's my quid pro quo." Yager crossed his arms like it was over.

Cat shook her head. "Well, that's a start, but you can do something else for him that won't cost you anything at all. In fact, you'll get a free meal out of it."

"Free meal?" Yager wrinkled his brow and kept his arms crossed.

"Wednesday, for lunch, you go to the Silver Liner. You have lunch, whatever you like, but preferably something his dad specializes in. Maybe the stuffed calamari." Cat threw her hands in the air. "Then, you *tweet* about how you love the Silver Liner and that's where you go before a game for your lucky calamari, or chicken sandwich, or whatever. Your three million followers then see you go four-for-four, and they go bonkers and suddenly *everyone* has to go to the Silver Liner for that famous calamari or whatever. Get it?"

A wave of excitement washed over Jalen.

He got it, but Yager was frowning.

37

IT WAS SO QUIET THEY COULD HEAR THE BIRDS twittering outside in the spring sunshine. It was a beautiful day, but Yager looked like a cloudburst.

"Like I said"—Yager was speaking to Jalen now—"I'm cutting you a break no matter what. That's my part. But . . . if this works? My foundation will pick up the travel team bill *and* I'll do the tweet. If it doesn't work? Well, then you got lucky to stay out of jail, and I'm going to buy a beach house on Nantucket or something. I decided against Tahiti."

"Why do you even say that?" Cat asked. "Jalen showed you he can do it. And if you tweet before it happens, then it'll be viral! Imagine it. . . ."

"I don't endorse things on Twitter," Yager said.

"Which is why it'd be so valuable," Cat countered. "Why we want it."

Jalen felt like they'd crossed a line, and he wanted to tell Cat to settle down, but he knew her well enough to know that there was no stopping her. And if it did work? He could only imagine what it would do for his father. Cat was brilliant.

"Look," Yager said, "this whole thing is crazy, but I'm at the end of my rope, and obviously I'll try anything. It could be a parlor trick or luck or I don't know what, but if Jalen can really tell me the pitches before they come, it'll be money. We still don't know if this can work, though, and we've got Jeffrey Foxx out there, who'll be doing everything he can to spoil it. So . . . *if* it works, then I'll tweet about the Silver Liner."

Cat and Yager stared each other down until Cat shrugged and, sounding cheery, said, "Okay, deal. Jalen is gonna show you. Oh, and you *will* eat there Wednesday and take the picture so you can tweet right after the game and people can see where your luck came from."

"From the calamari?" Yager was stone-faced.

"From the DeLucas," Cat said. "Jalen, his dad, the calamari. What's the diff? Oh, and we might have to talk about a contract if this works and you want Jalen to keep being your baseball genius. The first few weeks for letting him off, the Rockets' fee, and doing the tweet settles the score, but after that we need to negotiate in good faith. Just letting you know."

Yager couldn't help cracking a smile. "You should be an agent, you know that?"

"It's one of the possible things I'm thinking about," Cat said. "That or a talk show host or maybe president."

"That too," Yager said, standing.

Before Jalen could stop him, Daniel had his bottle of Yankee Stadium dirt out of his pocket, and he held it out to JY. "Would you mind signing this?"

Yager looked surprised, but he took the dirt before looking at Jalen. "Is this from the stadium?"

Jalen was horrified, but he whispered, "Yes. There was a little bit left in my pocket when I got home."

"Cat has one too!" Daniel blurted out.

Cat shot a scowl at Daniel.

To Jalen's surprise, Yager laughed and got a Sharpie from his kitchen, signing Daniel's bottle as well as Cat's, before saying, "The other thing we are going to do is keep all this quiet. Not the bottle of dirt, I mean Jalen. No newspaper reporters. No blogs. No tweeting about a baseball genius. Just some good old lucky calamari. The rest of this stays between us. Got it? I do *not* want Foxx to think this is some circus trick. He and the owner need to believe this comeback is all about me. That way they'll extend my contract, and I'll have a cushion."

Yager looked around with a hard stare, but when they all nodded, his face softened and he said, "Hey, I was about to hit a few balls. If you guys want, you can take a few swings. Interested?"

Daniel beamed. "You bet!"

"Sure." Jalen felt reluctant to return to the scene of his crime, but he couldn't resist the offer.

The Yankees star loosened up more after hitting, and he gave them both pointers that they had fresh in their minds when they showed up for their first Rockets practice that evening at the town field. Yager had Jalen lower his shoulder, and it really seemed to even out his swing. Yager had Daniel bring his bat back just a bit, and Daniel swore he could feel the added power.

Excited and ready, the two friends showed up at practice with dreams of greatness that were quickly dampened by their new teammates. The other boys all wore slick Nike gear. They had leather batting gloves, and their names were stitched into their fancy new bat bags. Except for a derisive snort from Chris Gamble, Jalen and Daniel were universally ignored, so they paired off and warmed up their arms alone until Coach Gamble blasted his whistle, bringing them all in around home plate.

The coach wore a red Rockets hat and hoodie, and cargo shorts that exposed a thick pair of legs so hairy that it almost looked like he was wearing really long socks. His big hands held a clipboard. A pen was behind his ear.

"First of all, congratulations to those of you who won the championship last night." The coach caught his son's eye and the two of them grinned, showing the same big white teeth. "That's what Rockets ball is all about. Champions. Those of you who don't know how to win . . . well, I hope I can teach you that."

Daniel made a soft farting sound with his lips.

"You have something to say, Mr. DeLuca?" Coach Gamble growled at Jalen, and Jalen knew he thought the noise had come from him instead of Daniel.

Jalen struggled to speak, knowing that this was not the way to start things with a guy like Coach Gamble.

He had to say something, and he had to say it fast.

38

"EXCUSE ME, COACH." DANIEL STEPPED FORWARD.
"Beef chips for lunch. That one snuck out."

Jalen let go a sigh of extreme relief. He was so grateful that Daniel had owned up to the noise, he wanted to hug him.

Half the team snickered, and to Jalen's surprise, the coach fought back a smile and shook his head before returning to his serious look. "Anyway, we are about winning. Everything I do is about winning, so those of you who are new to this team need to understand that what I say is like the word of God. You do not question me. You play where I say you'll play, and you play when I say you'll play. You don't complain, either. I've got a list as long as my arm of kids who want to be on this team. So I tell you to jump, you ask me, 'How high?'"

Coach Gamble glared all around before adding, "And that goes for what Coach Benning says as well."

Jalen hadn't really noticed the other adult. Mr. Benning was short and thick like his son, Dirk. He stepped out from behind Coach Gamble, wearing a red cap of his own, which he tipped to the players.

"Got that?" Coach Gamble shouted.

"Yes, Coach!" the team replied.

Coach Gamble blew his whistle and practice began. It was nothing like the low-key practices Coach Winkman conducted. The Rockets were highly organized, and there was no sitting around or loafing. It was all action: running, throwing, hitting, and catching. When they took a break halfway through, Jalen was thankful for the bottle of water he'd filled at the diner, and he slugged it down as he moved closer to Daniel, who'd plunked himself on the end of the bench.

"How'd the pitching go?" Jalen asked. He had been with Coach Benning doing fielding drills, while Daniel was with Coach Gamble and the other five pitchers.

Daniel took a drink from his Gatorade bottle and squinted at Jalen. "I should be the top dog, or at least number two behind Chris, but him and these two kids from Chappaqua got their noses so far up Coach Gamble's butt, I'll be lucky if I get more than an inning or two every weekend. I can read the writing on the wall."

Jalen felt a chill, because if Daniel wasn't going to be treated fairly, he doubted he would be either. There were eighteen players, and only nine could play at a time. That left plenty of room for benchwarmers.

"What'sa matter, Sandwich? You tired already?"

Jalen looked up and saw Chris standing there with Dirk Benning. They wore their flat-brimmed Rockets caps slightly crooked, and each had a bottle of blue Gatorade.

"Sandwich?" Jalen couldn't help sounding confused.

"Yeah." Chris took a long drink from his bottle but kept eye contact with Jalen. "Heard you had to make a bunch of sandwiches for my dad to even let you on this team."

Jalen's insides melted. Sick and horrified that everyone knew about his father's deal to make up the difference for his registration fee, he fought back his emotions.

"What's that?" Chris peered at him. "Sandwich Boy crying?"

"I'm not crying." Jalen stood up and glared right back at Chris.

"What you gonna do about it?" Chris jutted out his chin and tapped the sweet spot with his pointer finger. "Wanna hit me?"

Daniel was there between them and holding out his hands to keep them apart. "Hey, Chris, you ever take your fist and smash it right into a big hot pile of dog crap? You ever try that?"

Chris wrinkled his ugly face. "What's wrong with you?"

Daniel took Jalen by the arm now and led him away from the bench area, turning back to address the enormous pitcher. "Yeah, disgusting, right? Who wants hot poop all over his hand? That's why Jalen ain't gonna hit you, amigo."

Jalen was so mad, he almost couldn't smile. Almost.

They left Chris and Dirk there to figure it out. Then the whistle blew and they got back into action. By the time practice ended, the sun had dropped behind some clouds, and the late-spring light had faded. Coach Gamble gathered the team around him under the lights and told them to take a knee in the grass. Even Chris was huffing and bent over, and Jalen was hopeful he didn't have the energy to be mad.

"Okay," Coach Gamble said to them. "Not bad for the first night, but we've got a lot of work to do before Saturday. We'll go again tomorrow. I'm out of town Wednesday, but plan on being here Thursday, same time, to sharpen up before the tournament. I'll give you Friday off to rest."

Now Jalen had a new reason for being sick.

Thursday evening he was supposed to be at Yankee Stadium.

"The schedule will change depending on my own work schedule and the field availability, but you need to know that I'm gonna own this seven-to-nine time slot of your lives for the entire summer and every minute of the weekends as well. This weekend's different because the tournament is right in White Plains, so you'll sleep at home, but normally, we'll be traveling Friday afternoons. That's the commitment it takes to be a Rocket. I'm sure you all know that, but if you have a problem, now would be the time to tell me."

Jalen wanted to raise his hand and tell the coach he'd need to miss Thursday to save JY's career, that he'd be sitting right next to the dugout, field level, in the owner's seats at Yankee Stadium. He wanted to do that, but he didn't know if he could or should, and he kept quiet.

After a team break with a "Champions!" chant, Jalen walked with Daniel off the field.

"What are you gonna do about Thursday?" Daniel asked.

"I gotta get past Wednesday first," Jalen said.

"Yeah, but you will, and then what?"

Jalen sighed and looked at his feet. "I have no idea."

39

THE NEXT DAY, TUESDAY, JALEN HAD A HARD TIME concentrating in school, but things were winding down anyway since they were nearing the end of the year.

At lunch Cat showed him a text she'd received from her mom, asking if Jalen could meet with JY at four p.m.

"Wow," Daniel said. "He must want to go over your secret signals. Totally cool."

Jalen stopped eating his meat loaf sandwich on fresh Italian bread. "Why is he asking her to ask you to ask me?"

"Well . . ." Cat fiddled with her bag of chips before looking up. "You don't have a phone, Jalen. It's hard to get hold of you."

Jalen bit his lip.

"Maybe, if we get this genius thing going, we'll negotiate a phone for you." Cat sounded excited.

Jalen nodded. "Well, ask him if he can pick me up at the diner. I've got to help my dad after school, and tell him I've got to be back at seven p.m. for practice, too. Daniel, can you pick up my equipment bag for me?"

"Consider it done."

Cat typed under the table because phones weren't allowed in school, even though the only time anyone got in trouble was if they had it out on their desk in the middle of a class or sat in the front row of desks and couldn't keep their eyes off it.

Cat looked up. "Got it. You're all set."

Jalen threw his Yager meeting into the pot of things to be worried about and stewed the rest of the day. When he arrived at the Silver Liner, Gretta and Jimmy were standing behind the counter with their arms folded, looking miffed. There wasn't a customer in the place.

"What's up, guys?" Jalen asked, heading for the kitchen door.

"You can't go in there." Gretta chewed the black-painted fingernail on her pinky and forced a smile. "You think we're out here for kicks?"

"Why not?" Jalen paused with his hand on the door.

"Some hotshot lawyer or something," said Jimmy, scratching his pale tattooed belly. "Or a banker. They all look the same."

Jalen hesitated, then went in and nearly got knocked over by a big man in a suit, carrying a briefcase in one hand. The man didn't even try to catch Jalen, but he staggered upright by the sink. The man did turn toward Jalen's father's office, though, to say, "I'm sorry, Fabio. You had a pretty good run. Most restaurants go under in the first two years. You've been here how long? Eleven?"

The man turned and left, and Jalen froze at the look on his father's face. "Dad? Is everything okay?"

Without words, his father's face said *disaster*.

40

JALEN'S FATHER ROCKED FORWARD SO THAT HIS
desk chair squeaked, and he buried his face in his hands
for a moment before looking up and forcing a smile. "I
know we don't talk about her, but your mother . . ."

The word hung there, suspended in silence.

His father cleared his throat. "She had to go. Her
family, they didn't want her to marry me in the first place.
Then . . . then things happened and she had a chance she
always dreamed of, and I said she had to go. She worried
about you, but I said to her, 'Jalen, he's gonna be fine. He's
my boy and you know I'm gonna take good care of him.
I swear on my own life he's gonna be fine.'" His father's
smile broke apart. He turned his eyes toward a pile of

papers on his desk that looked like bills, and tears spilled down his cheeks. He bit into his knuckle. "But now . . . I don't know how good a job I've done. . . ."

Jalen crossed the floor and bent down and hugged his dad tight. His father's thick shoulders shook. Jalen held on until his father took a deep breath and sniffed and gently pushed him to arm's length. "I don't have to own a restaurant. I can get a job in a pizza shop and we can get an apartment. Not big, but we don't need big. We're gonna be okay, Jalen. I swear we're gonna be okay."

His father stood up and gave Jalen another quick hug and a kiss on the top of his head before he said, "Don't tell Gretta and Jimmy. We've got the diner until end of the month, and I don't want the food to be bad. It's gotta be good to the end, and they won't work if they know. *Capisce?*"

"Okay, Dad." Jalen nodded. He wanted more than anything to tell him about James Yager and the tweet that could save them. He wanted to, but he knew that the only thing worse than losing the diner for his dad would be to give him hope that he might not lose it and then lose it anyway. That might kill him.

So Jalen got to work, helping his father prepare a fish stew that made his stomach rumble as it simmered on the stove. When the work was done, Jalen looked at the clock. "Dad, I gotta go, okay?"

"You got homework?" his father asked.

"Actually, I gotta help James Yager," Jalen said.

"Mr. Yager? I thought you going to help him tomorrow night, at the game?" His father began chopping some garlic, and it filled the air with its pungent smell.

Jalen nodded. "Right. Yes. But I need to signal him if I know the pitch and what pitch it is."

The big knife in his father's hand stopped. "Jalen . . . is this really a thing you can do? I don't know. I don't know. . . ."

"I think I can, Dad," Jalen said. "I said I'd try."

"Okay, Jalen." His father looked down at the cutting board and began to chop again. The staccato rhythm sounded like a woodpecker. "You do that. You try."

41

THE BLACK LAMBORGHINI THUNDERED UP AND
Jalen hopped in without looking back at the diner. Instead
of turning up the hill toward Old Post Road, they went
straight through the middle of town, with small shop windows buzzing by at light speed so they could beat a yellow
traffic signal.

"Where we going?" Jalen asked as they veered onto the
highway.

"The city." Yager switched stations on the radio until he
had an old Prince song that he began to hum along with.

"The stadium again?" Jalen figured Yager was nervous
about the sight lines and wanted to test out their signals,
a kind of dry run.

"Uh . . . no." Yager swerved through two cars like a rocket. "It's a surprise."

Jalen nodded like he got surprises all the time, but inside he was boiling with curiosity. They got off the thruway and onto the West Side Highway, exiting at 72nd Street. Through a canyon of buildings blocking out the sky they went until they reached a line of trees that extended both ways as far as Jalen could see. "What's that?"

Yager took a right and glanced at him. "Central Park. You've never been here?"

Jalen shook his head. "No."

"It's pretty amazing. Woods, ponds, ball fields, paths to walk, playgrounds. When I first came to New York, I had a place near here. Walked through that park all the time."

"By yourself?" Jalen asked.

Yager snorted and went quiet for a minute, pausing to allow a woman on a bicycle the time to make a turn. "No. I used to have a girlfriend, but that's a whole other story, and we're here."

He pulled the car up in front of a building overlooking the park, and they got out.

The doorman wore a crimson hat and a coat with gold braiding. He seemed to recognize Yager and asked him how long he'd be.

"Not long. Twenty minutes maybe."

Jalen followed Yager into the fancy building. People coming in and out mostly wore suits and ties or dresses with high heels. Yager didn't seem to mind being in a T-shirt and jeans, so Jalen figured he was okay in the sweatpants and T-shirt he had on for practice. Up they went in a shiny elevator that moved so fast it reminded Jalen of the Lamborghini. When they got off, Yager led them down a long hallway and knocked on a wide mahogany door. It swung open, and a young woman led them into a living room that looked out over much of the city. The woman quickly disappeared.

Jalen felt like he was on a cloud.

Then he heard someone behind them say, "James!"

Jalen turned to look and couldn't believe his eyes.

42

THE MAN HUGGING JAMES YAGER LOOKED LIKE
Derek Jeter, but he was taller and leaner than Jalen
thought he'd be, and his head was closely shaved.

Jalen waited until the man stood directly in front of him
with a hand extended to shake before he decided that it
definitely was Jeter.

"So you're the baseball genius?" Jeter's pale-green eyes
were warm and kind, and Jalen felt like he was somehow
talking to an old friend instead of a superstar.

He heard himself say, "I guess so," and felt ridiculous.

Jeter smiled, though, then nodded and looked at Yager.
"So, let's see."

They followed the Yankees icon into another room,

where a huge flat-screen TV played a baseball game. "The Tampa-Arizona game started at three forty, so . . ." Jeter clicked his remote and scrolled through the satellite guide until Rubby De La Rosa appeared atop the mound, winding up and delivering a strike. "Let's sit. I'd like to see what you can do, Jalen. Okay?"

"Okay. Sure." Jalen felt his voice shaking, but he sat down next to Jeter, giving him plenty of space. Yager stood with his arms crossed.

"Can I watch a little, first?" Jalen asked.

"Sure," said Jeter.

De La Rosa gave up a single to Corey Dickerson before striking out Souza. Jeter looked at Jalen curiously and patiently asked, "Anything yet?"

Jalen bit his lip. "Uh . . . maybe."

De La Rosa wound up. Jalen knew it was a fastball but didn't say anything.

"If you think this is pressure, we have no shot tomorrow night, I can tell you that." Yager began to pace, and he looked at Jeter hard. "See? I knew this was too crazy."

Jalen watched and thought *fastball* again, so he just said it. "Fastball."

Fastball it was. Longoria let it go for a strike. Jeter and Yager looked at each other.

"Yeah, but De La Rosa throws that pitch three out of four times." Yager stopped and stroked his neck.

"Okay," said Jeter, "so we keep watching."

"Fastball again," Jalen said.

It was. Longoria fouled it.

"And another fastball," Jalen said.

Longoria let it go. The pitch was high and a ball. Jalen's stomach rolled over because it was too many fastballs. De La Rosa had to throw something else, but that wasn't what Jalen felt.

"Fastball."

"Jeez." Yager threw up his hands, but it was a fastball Longoria fouled again. "Can Rubby throw anything else?"

"I don't know on a one-two count. That's his money." Jeter sounded totally relaxed. Jalen envied him.

The camera went off De La Rosa, showing a close-up of Diamondbacks manager Chip Hale, because the announcers were talking about him.

"I hate when they do this," Jalen blurted out. "Show the *action*."

Jeter chuckled, but the pitch went without a call from Jalen, a slider that struck Longoria out.

"Good God." Yager dug his fingers into his own dark hair.

"Relax." Jeter sat back into the couch. "I'm good till five forty-five."

"Easy for you to say," Yager said. "This is it for me. I can't believe I even took it this far. I'm sorry, Derek. I won't waste your time anymore. It's over. Come on, kid.

"I'm pulling the plug."

43

JETER WAS UP ON HIS FEET, AND HE PUT A HAND
on Yager's arm. "Wait, James. Just wait a minute. You
know how I always say not to complicate things by thinking too much about what other people might think? That's
what you're doing. Who cares how crazy this sounds? I
don't know everything that's out there in the world, and
neither do you. Let's see if Jalen can do this. Give him a
chance."

Yager shook his head and rubbed his eyes. "Okay.
Thanks."

The two players sat on either side of Jalen.

"Okay," Jeter said, pointing to the screen. "Let's do this."

Jalen took a deep breath. "Fastball."

It was.

The next pitch was as well, and the next. Yager sighed, but Jalen kept his eyes on the screen.

"Changeup," Jalen said.

De La Rosa threw a changeup.

"Curve," said Jalen.

A curve it was. Logan Forsythe hit it, putting two on.

"Hey, hey." Jeter patted Jalen on the back, flooding him with warmth.

"Fastball."

It was.

"Slider."

It was.

"Changeup."

Miller struck out, ending the inning.

"Yup." Jeter stood up, clicked off the TV, and looked at Yager with a serious face. "He's real."

"Just like that?" Yager's mouth hung open.

"Yeah, James." Jeter pointed to the darkened screen. "He did it. Exactly what you told me he could do on the phone."

"But . . . you don't want to see more?" Yager asked. "It could be luck."

Jeter turned to Jalen. "Can you do that all the time, or was it luck?"

Jalen stuttered. "I—uh—yes, I can do it."

"You think this kid would lie?" Jeter chuckled and thumped Yager on the back like he'd just hit a home run. "Come on. Don't be afraid."

"Afraid?" Yager stiffened.

"Yeah," Jeter said. "Sometimes people are. Sometimes you get exactly what you need, and you're afraid because it seems too good to be true. Don't do that, James. Let it be that good. Get out there tomorrow night and knock it out of the park. I'll be watching."

"You're coming to the game?" Yager wrinkled his face.

Jeter laughed and pointed to the TV. "No. You know I hate being there without a bat in my hand. I'll watch, though. Promise."

"Okay, well . . ." Yager still seemed uncertain, but he hugged his friend. "Thanks. I really, really appreciate it."

"No problem."

Jalen followed Yager out of the room, and Jeter saw them to the front door. Jalen couldn't help stealing another look at the incredible view.

"Hey Jalen," Jeter said at the door.

"Yes, sir?"

"Have fun."

"Fun?" Jalen scowled, trying to figure out what the star ballplayer meant.

"Yeah." Jeter smiled a bright-white smile. "I mean, it's a gift, right? That thing you do. Enjoy it. Have fun."

Jalen's face relaxed, and he nodded and shook Jeter's hand one more time before they left. A daze clouded his mind until the sign ROCKTON 10 MILES jumped out at him from the roadside. Jalen felt a sudden panic when he looked at the clock and it said 17:43. He did a quick calculation, subtracting twelve from seventeen and getting 5:43. He let out a sigh, but then furrowed his brow because he had no idea how they could be back so fast.

"Wait, is that really the time?" Jalen pointed across the steering wheel at the glowing numbers on the other side of the speedometer, where the needle floated between eighty and ninety.

Yager glanced down. "Uh . . . let's see . . . no, I forgot to adjust it to daylight savings. I hate that daylights savings. It should really say eighteen forty-three."

"That's . . ." Jalen bolted upright in his seat. "That's six forty-three, now six forty-four. I've got practice at seven!"

"Well . . ." Yager shrugged. "A couple minutes won't matter, right?"

Jalen's eyes widened. "Oh, yes it will. I can't be late. I *can't*."

"I can't go much faster." Yager swerved smoothly between two cars.

"Oh no. Oh no." Jalen felt his insides turn to mush. "That stupid traffic in the city. I *can't* be late. You promised. I'll lose my spot. I can't believe you did this!"

"Hey, easy, kid," Yager said. "Relax."

"I can't relax. You don't understand. This is all your fault!" Jalen pounded a fist on the dashboard. "You don't believe me? Why? I keep showing you, and now you're going to ruin everything!"

Yager frowned, downshifted the car, and surged ahead. Speed pressed Jalen back into the seat, and he pointed the way to Simon Park once they soared off the highway. When Yager pulled over before the entrance to the park, Jalen's mouth fell open. "What are you doing?"

Yager shook his head. "I can't let them see me."

"You . . ." Jalen was so furious he couldn't speak.

"You better run," Yager said, nodding at the clock, which read 6:59. "I'll see you at the diner tomorrow about three thirty."

All the problems in Jalen's life piled up behind a dam in his mind: his dad making sandwiches and the bank taking the diner, Chris Gamble hating him, and him missing Thursday's practice, but first and foremost was being late right now. Jalen wanted to explode and somehow force Yager to drive right into the park. What did it matter if people knew he was a baseball genius, the kid who would save Yager's career? They'd find out eventually, wouldn't they?

No matter what he might say, though, Jalen could clearly read the look on Yager's face. The ballplayer wasn't going to budge. So Jalen flung the door open and took off, praying Coach Gamble's watch was slow.

44

JALEN SUCKED AIR THROUGH HIS DRY MOUTH.
His lungs burned, and he sprinted the last fifty yards
when he heard Coach Gamble's whistle and the rest of
the team circled up. Daniel looked at him with wide eyes
and a lower lip pinned under his teeth.

"You barely made it, DeLuca." The giant coach looked
up from his watch and cast a dirty look at Jalen before
addressing the team. "Okay. Day two. A lot like day one,
only we'll do some live pitching to end things. One line
behind home plate, let's go!"

Jalen fell in with his teammates and ran the bases,
gasping for breath and stumbling across home plate on
the last lap. They went right to a long-toss drill to loosen

up their arms, and Jalen found himself next to Chris.

"You're hanging by a thread, Sandwich." Chris threw the ball without looking at Jalen. "I can feel it. You won't make it more than two weeks, is my bet."

Jalen gritted his teeth. He ached to tell this big jerk where he'd just been—Derek Jeter's hotel suite—and what he was about to do—save the career of the Yankees' star second baseman—but there was nothing he could say.

"What?" Chris snatched the ball Dirk threw to him out of the air. "You got nothing to say? You only write notes and stick them on people's backs, huh? I figured."

Jalen tried to focus on his skills. He wanted to make himself better. He felt certain he needed to be much better than anyone else if he was going to break into the Rockets lineup. It was no use, though. Jalen couldn't concentrate. He muffed pop flies and dropped throws. His own tosses were off target, and by the time he stepped up to the plate at the end of practice, he was a bundle of nerves. Of course it wasn't Daniel or another less-skilled pitcher Jalen had to face. It was Chris atop the mound, casting multiple shadows beneath the field lights shining above.

The idea of somehow pulling himself out of his funk by smacking several pitches over the fence quickly disappeared. Even though Jalen knew each and every pitch he was going to get, his timing was off. After the first couple of strikes, he let his shoulder rise up again, cursing the advice Yager had given him. Two more fastballs screamed by him, with his bat whistling in the wind, before he lowered his shoulder again. Chris's grin grew and grew until it looked like his face must be hurting.

Ten pitches were what each player got from a live pitcher.

Jalen didn't hit a single one of his, not even a foul ball, not even a tick.

He thumped the bat on the ground and marched back to the dugout to get his glove and take a spot in the field. He tried to ignore the soft chuckling from Chris, atop the mound, as he jogged out into the outfield.

Daniel stepped up to the plate next and blasted seven out of ten, confirming that Chris wasn't invincible. After two more batters, Coach Gamble blew his whistle and brought everyone into a circle at home plate. He checked his clipboard and looked up. "Okay, not a bad night. Thursday, same time. Those of you who struggled hitting tonight might want to see if you can get to the Pro Swing in White Plains. . . ."

Jalen expected the coach to make eye contact with him and he braced himself for it, relieved that it didn't come. They all put their hands in for a chant and broke to the cry of, "Champions!"

Jalen hung his head and headed for the dugout along with everyone else. He had nearly reached his equipment bag when he heard someone call his name.

Jalen turned and saw that it was Coach Benning. He and Coach Gamble stood at home plate, right where Jalen had left them. Coach Benning crooked his finger and Jalen returned.

Coach Gamble scowled down at him. "Jalen, we need to talk. Coach Benning and I aren't sure this is working out."

45

JALEN COULD HEAR THE CRICKETS CHIRPING
among the trees where the picnic tables stood and the thunk
of car doors as his teammates got swallowed up by their
rides. The two men looked at each other, Coach Benning
squinting up at Coach Gamble in the thin light with a nod.
Their boys had disappeared somewhere, and Jalen wondered if they were watching from some secret spot.

"Well . . ." Coach Gamble cleared his throat and touched
the brim of his cap. "You almost did us all a favor and
showed up late. That would've made things easy, because
we don't bend our rules."

The coaches looked at each other in obvious agreement.

Coach Gamble turned back to Jalen to study his face.

"You look upset, Jalen, and we don't want you to be upset."

Jalen stiffened at the sound of Coach Gamble's softened voice, certain that something bad was sure to follow.

"It's just that . . ." Here Coach Gamble seemed to pass the baton of speaking to Coach Benning.

"You know this team is all about winning," said Coach Benning.

Coach Gamble nodded. "It's *all* about winning. That's the only thing, and we know it wasn't—isn't—an easy thing for your dad from a money standpoint and . . . to be honest?" Coach Gamble paused, forcing a smile. "You want me to be honest, right, Jalen?"

Jalen could only dip his head. Somehow the two coaches being nice to him created more discomfort than if they were growling with anger.

"Right, and well, sometimes you play outside yourself," Coach Gamble continued. "And that's what I think happened last week when you played us, the A's. You played *outside* yourself and made an impression."

"A very good impression," said Coach Benning.

"An excellent impression," said Coach Gamble.

Jalen looked up at the enormous man and saw that the wiry hairs in his nose had been cut back. He could still see them, though, lurking beneath the shadow of his nostrils and somehow looking even more dangerous.

"But now," Coach Gamble continued, "after a couple practices, we see that your skills aren't really up to the rest of these guys and—with the money situation and your dad having to make all those sandwiches—we thought we'd give you a chance to get your money back. It's not too late."

Jalen felt the earth shifting beneath his feet. "You . . . don't want me?"

"Oh, we *want* you." Coach Benning nodded furiously. "But it doesn't seem like it's going to be all that good of an experience for you."

"We think you'll struggle," Coach Benning added.

Jalen's face felt like he'd gotten too many shots from the dentist. He felt like he should know what they meant, but they were saying one thing when it also seemed like they meant something else. His thoughts were muddled by the horror of being kicked off the team when he'd made it on time after all. He hadn't even asked to skip Thursday night yet. "You don't think I'm good enough," Jalen said, "but you'll keep me anyway? As long as I don't break the rules?"

"We wanted you to know that you still could get your money back because we really don't know how much playing time you're going to get this summer." Coach Gamble seemed relieved to have his cards out on the table.

Jalen bit his lip. They'd actually hoped he'd be late. If he was late, they could have gotten rid of him without a problem, but the reason they didn't want him was because they thought he wasn't good enough. He *was* good enough. He just needed a calmer head to prove it. He saw a clear path, too. If he helped James Yager, he'd get the tweet that would save his father's business. Also, Yager would be so overjoyed, he and Jalen would be even. Jalen's cloud of guilt over everything that had happened would be blown away. With a clear head, he'd be back to his normal self on the baseball diamond.

He just needed to hang on.

"Well," Jalen said after pretending to think about it, "I'd like to stay."

"He'd like to stay." Coach Gamble looked at Coach Benning like the other man had done something wrong.

"Yes," Coach Benning said. "That's what he said."

"But you don't have to tell us right now." Coach Gamble put a beefy hand on Jalen's shoulder and gave it a gentle squeeze. "You need to take more time to think about something this important. Maybe talk to your dad? The money and all . . ."

Jalen knew they weren't going to take his answer, so he stayed quiet.

They all stood silently in a pool of discomfort until

Coach Gamble angled his head toward the backstop. "Okay, Jalen. That's it. We need to go over some things, so you can get on your way. We'll see you Thursday. Don't be late." His voice had gone from falsely pleasant to gruff.

Jalen could see the blue pickup truck Daniel's father drove waiting for him in the parking lot. The orange moon of Daniel's face stared at Jalen through the glare of the window and he walked toward the truck, thinking about Thursday.

As he reached for the truck door to make his getaway, Jalen realized there was really nothing to worry about, because he had to get past tomorrow first.

46

JALEN HELPED AT THE DINER UNTIL HE COULD
barely keep his eyes open and his father ordered him
home, where he lay down on top of his bed without getting undressed.

When he woke, it was to an earthquake of vibration
and noise. The four a.m. train rarely did more than cause
him to roll over. This time it woke him from a dream of
bankers swarming the infield, and Coach Gamble holler-
ing that his swing was late.

"If you can't get a hit, you can't make the team!" his
coach bellowed at him from a lawn chair atop the dugout,
while Chris ate onion rings and sneered at Jalen from the
dugout below. The dream-words rang in Jalen's ears as

the trembling settled and the train eased into the station. After a few minutes, it hissed and tooted twice. Five hundred tons of train crept away. More crossing bells rang as it picked up speed, and then a warning horn sounded as it flashed through town. Jalen tried to go back to sleep, but the blare of the horn faded like a mistaken warning cry amid the now-distant clatter of crossing bells. It was a haunting sound that stayed in his mind, warning of some trouble ahead.

Jalen got up in the dark, wide awake.

He ran the water in the sink and brushed his teeth. The puffy-eyed boy in the mirror didn't look like someone who could save a baseball career, not even his own, let alone a famous Yankee player's.

Jalen slipped on his shoes and went out the back. He walked the tracks to the diner, where the newspaper lay like a dead fish on the steps. Jalen looked around for any sign of the guy who delivered it. Puffs of breath left his mouth, glowing in the streetlight before going the way of real ghosts. Jalen could smell the Dumpster from where he stood, and he fretted over whether they'd pick up the trash before Yager stopped by before the game to have his photo taken with a plate of stuffed calamari.

He returned home, tiptoeing inside with a shiver. In the narrow front room—which was kitchen, dining area, and living room all rolled into one—he took up his spot in a rickety chair whose faded cushion provided minimum comfort but offered the best reading light there was to be had. He pored over the sports section, seeing that Derek Holton would be the pitcher Yager would have to face. Jalen scowled, wondering why everything had to go against him. Holton was the White Sox's ace. He was a lefty who hid the ball and threw high heat with a rear sidearm motion. Holton had more horizontal movement on his fastball than Randy Johnson, and a lot of people said his slider was his nastiest pitch. For Yager, as a right-handed batter, that slider would be like an outside pitch at the belt that could cross the inside of the plate at his knees. Holton was a beast.

Jalen closed his eyes and—like magic—there it was, a billboard busy with a million numbers and graphs in his brain, every stat and tendency Derek Holton had generated since he'd entered professional baseball. He didn't visualize it to study but rather to assure himself it was all there, and it was. He didn't want to think about how it all worked; it just did, and the times he'd tried to name it were the times he'd stumbled and crumbled and failed. Thinking about it too much, and certainly trying to study it, ruined everything.

In fourth grade, Mrs. Boehr said he was off the charts for the state math test they'd taken as a practice before the real thing. With great joy and trembling hands, she informed Jalen that he might be a savant. Jalen didn't want to be a savant. He wanted to be a second baseman for the Yankees, and Mrs. Boehr's excitement had scared him because adults weren't supposed to be silly with glee. The next week a man with a thick gray beard and glasses appeared to take Jalen out of class for more tests.

Jalen watched the man from the corner of his eye as he selected the answers to the problems before him on a multiple-choice exam. He could tell they were supposed to get harder and harder, but the first was as easy as the next. The man's eyes got wide and his foot began to tap the floor after Jalen got number 23 correct. Jalen heard the man whisper, "Yes!" to himself and pump his fist, and that scared him. After that, Jalen was careful to answer incorrectly, even after the man made him stop and look him directly in the eyes.

"Now, are you *sure*?" the man asked.

Jalen was sure. He was sure he didn't want that kind of attention for something as stuffy as math. He didn't intend to end up at a desk crunching numbers for the rest of his life. He intended to be outdoors, smacking doubles and home runs and snagging jaw-dropping line drives.

He liked Mrs. Boehr, and it hurt to disappoint her, especially when she sat him down and explained what a great gift it was to be different. But Jalen already knew better than that. Being different was only to your advantage if it was because you were tremendously better than everyone else at sports.

Still, there it was, all those numbers floating in his brain, all coming together with the certainty of two plus two equaling four when he was out there on the baseball diamond.

He put the newspaper down and went through the signals he and Yager had devised. He only needed four for Holton: slider, sinker, changeup, and four-seam fastball. He went over the others, too, for whatever relief pitcher they'd see, but he focused on Holton's toolbox. Four-seam was easy, four fingers. Sinker was a thumb pointing down, a pitch that came in flat only to drop at the last moment. Changeup was two thumbs-up. And the slider was a throat-cutting motion, because that was Yager's least favorite pitch to hit, even though he could hit them all.

The five a.m. train wailed, approaching fast. The crossing bells began to clang, and the house shook a bit. Jalen plugged his ears until things quieted down and then made some breakfast as the train left Rockton behind in a powerful silence.

School was a blur and before he knew it, Jalen was stepping off the bus with Daniel and Cat shadowing him. Yager's car already rested outside the empty diner at an angle that took up two parking spots.

"He's early." Jalen fretted more to himself than his

friends. He sniffed the air and his stomach turned at the ripe smell of garbage. "You've got to be kidding me. I'd like to strangle that garbageman."

Daniel sniffed as well. "It's not too bad."

Jalen checked himself from reminding Daniel that he lived over a stable, but he was so mad he felt he had to say something. "The only thing worse could be a clogged toilet."

"Or Chris Gamble's breath." Daniel burst into a smile Jalen just couldn't return.

They went through the front door and found Yager at table seven, with a plate of stuffed calamari drowned in steaming red sauce. Jalen's father stood beside him, wiping his hands on his apron, obviously eager to see the star's reaction.

"Ahhh! There you are!" Jalen's father welcomed them with open arms. "I told Mr. Yager you'd be getting off the bus any second. Who's gonna take the picture? Cat?"

Cat stepped forward with her phone, and Yager picked up his knife and fork, cutting into a piece of squid. Cat began snapping pictures. Yager let the bite cool, and he blew on it a couple of times before he put it in his mouth and began to chew. He chewed and chewed, and Jalen got nervous.

Yager closed his eyes and swallowed. Then, keeping his eyes shut, he opened his mouth to speak.

Jalen had no idea what was going to come out.

47

"DELICIOUS." THE YANKEES STAR SPOKE SO
softly that Jalen had to look at Daniel's face to see if he'd
heard it correctly. Daniel's face lit up, and he gave Jalen
a high five.

"Let me see a thumbs-up." Cat was working the phone,
moving all around for different angles. "That's it, big
smile. Now cutting into it."

Yager ignored Cat. He continued to eat, closing his
eyes as he swallowed each bite until nothing was left.
Finally he set the silverware down on his plate. "How
are you going to choose? You must've taken a thousand
pictures."

Cat looked at her phone. "No, only ninety-seven."

Yager laughed, and Jalen's dad joined in.

"So," Jalen's dad said, "you like?"

"No." Yager looked at Jalen's dad with a straight face. "I *love*."

"Ha-ha! Jalen! He loves my *nonna*'s stuffed calamari!" Jalen's dad clasped his hand, pulling Jalen into a hug. Jalen wanted to say something about the bank, but he didn't want to jinx everything. Nothing was guaranteed; Jalen had to deliver. Yager had to go four-for-four at the plate, and *then* he'd tweet about the Silver Liner. Yager had been firm on that.

"I'll get more for you kids. Everyone's gonna have lucky calamari!" Jalen's dad disappeared into the kitchen.

The three friends sat down around Yager. Cat scrolled through her pictures, showing the Yankees player the ones she thought he should use until Jalen's father reappeared with four smoking plates. Jalen swallowed. He wasn't hungry in the least.

Yager held up a hand. "No more, Fabio. I have to play, and I'm going to be late to batting practice."

"You come later then," Jalen's dad said. "Is just as good when I heat it up. Some say better. Jalen likes the calamari the second day even better."

Yager stood up, and Jalen's dad offered him a linen napkin. "For you face. The red sauce, she's a little spilled."

Yager wiped his face and sighed heavily, looking at Jalen. "Okay. You ready?"

"Sure." Jalen wished he was half as ready as he sounded, and he didn't think he sounded all that ready. The pressure was already killing him.

"My mom won't be here until four." Cat looked at her watch.

"Yeah, I know." Yager looked worried. "I wish I could take you with me, but I don't want Foxx to think you all are anything but fans. Ideally, he won't even know you're there, but I think he's pretty observant."

"Guy's a genius, from what they say," Daniel piped up. "So that would make sense."

"He's not a genius like Jalen." Cat seemed offended, and Jalen remembered the GM's angry red face and bow tie.

"No, I didn't mean that," Daniel said. "No one's like Jalen."

Jalen warmed with pride.

"Speaking of Foxx," JY said, reaching into his pocket, "I got these for you."

Yager held out a pair of mirrored wraparound sunglasses. "I think they'll fit, and they'll keep people from seeing you focus nonstop on the pitcher. It's a little thing, but little things make the difference between winning and losing."

Jalen took the glasses and tried them on. "Thanks."

"Okay, so . . . here we go." JY held out a hand to Jalen, and as Jalen shook it, he realized the star was nervous. "I'll see you guys at the stadium. You got the signals?"

Jalen nodded. He set his fork down and ran through them quick and clean. Yager seemed at a loss for words. He stared at Jalen for a moment and muttered something to himself before saying, "Good." Then he turned and walked away.

Jalen removed the sunglasses and pushed his food around on his plate, not hungry at all.

"That was weird," Daniel said.

"He's at the edge of the abyss." Cat followed Yager with her eyes, watching until his car pulled away.

"That sounds like something out of a book," Daniel said. "What's it mean in English?"

"The abyss is an endless nothingness," Cat said, "like dark space."

"What's that have to do with baseball?" Daniel took a sip from his water glass.

Jalen spoke up. "The end of life as he knows it. If he doesn't turn things around, he won't be a baseball player anymore."

"JY's still got his mansion and his dogs," Daniel said. "And he was talking about getting a place on a beach somewhere. That doesn't sound like the end to me. I mean, gosh. I want to play pro ball too. Don't tell me when it's over your life is an abyss. That stinks."

"Despite what you think," Cat said, "it's true. Anyway, Jalen is gonna fix it, aren't you, Jalen?"

Jalen stood up and automatically began to clear the table. "That's the plan." He didn't want to tell them that there was more at stake than Yager's career. He didn't want to talk about how he needed that tweet to save the Silver Liner from the bank. The pressure was building inside him, and he didn't want Daniel reminding him about what was in the balance.

Jalen cleaned up, then helped his dad in the kitchen while Daniel and Cat argued among themselves until Cat's mom pulled up in her white Range Rover. They rode without talking much, and before Jalen knew it they were pulling into a parking garage beside the stadium. The streets were crowded with Yankee fans, almost everyone wearing navy blue and white. Many wore their favorite player's number on pinstriped jerseys. Jalen felt like he and his friends stuck out in their school clothes. Only Cat's mom had the right colors, with her dark jeans and a blue sweater. They wove their way through the crowd to the will call gate and waited in an area blocked off by velvet ropes.

Jalen trembled with excitement and nerves as they stepped up to the window behind Cat's mom. He tried to focus on the opportunity, not what he might lose. He had to think positive.

"Hewlett." Cat's mom spoke loudly through the speaker in the glass as she slipped her driver's license into the metal tray beneath it. "Victoria Hewlett. Four tickets."

The balding man behind the counter worked on his computer and frowned. "You said Hewlett? With an *H*?"

His voice buzzed coming through the speaker.

"Yes," Cat's mom said.

The man nodded and got up. There was a file folder on a shelf behind him. A supervisor came over to the man, and Jalen watched them talking through the glass. They went through the folder but took nothing out.

Finally the supervisor came to the window. "Did you say Hewlett?"

"Yes," Cat's mom said. "Victoria Hewlett. With an *H*."

"Could it be under another name?" the man asked.

Cat's mom looked at Jalen. "Maybe DeLuca?"

"Okay, we'll try that." The man returned to the folder file and went through it.

Jalen had that sinking feeling he got when a teacher announced a pop spelling quiz. He couldn't help thinking of Jeffrey Foxx, the GM, a man Jalen knew was smart enough to figure things out and who he could imagine was devious enough to do something with the tickets so they couldn't get in. Jalen didn't like to predict things in real life as he did on the baseball field, but sometimes that happened too.

Other people came and went to the windows on either side of them. Finally the supervisor returned to the window and said, "Sorry, ma'am. We don't have any tickets for you."

48

DESPITE EVERYTHING THAT WAS ON THE LINE,
Jalen felt strangely relieved.

"That's impossible." Cat's mom wasn't backing down, and she set her feet like she was there to stay.

The supervisor looked at the line of people behind her. He ran a hand through his hair and it stuck out like a madman's. "What credit card did you use to buy these tickets?"

"We didn't *buy* these tickets," she said. "James Yager left them for us."

The man's face relaxed. "Ohhh. You're at the *will call* window, ma'am. You want the VIP window. That's near Gate Four."

The man pointed. "Go out and around. They'll have your tickets there."

Jalen took a deep breath and followed Cat's mom through the crowd again. The VIP line was short and flowed quickly inside to the entryway where Jalen had been with the police. Babe Ruth, wearing his enormous crown, smiled down. Cat's mom surrendered her purse for inspection and a man swept a wand over them one at a time. There was a counter that Jalen hadn't noticed the last time. A woman behind it quickly produced their tickets, then fixed paper wristbands onto each of them.

They boarded the elevator with a handful of other people, some dressed in Yankees gear, some in nice clothes. Daniel's eyes were wide, and he looked like he was eager to say something. Cat and her mom, though, were cool and calm. They went left instead of right out of the elevator and into the VIP Club's large dining area. Buffet stations had more food than people. Carved meat steamed beneath bright lights, and bowls of colorful side dishes waited for people with inviting silver tongs beside them.

"Can we eat this stuff?" Daniel's whisper was laced with awe.

"Of course. Are you hungry?" Cat's mom asked.

"No, but I could put some in my pockets for later."

"Uh, no. There'll be plenty of food later on, too," Cat's mom said. "Jalen looks like he'd rather sit down."

"We ate at the diner," Cat said. "Jalen's dad made us calamari."

"Then sit down it is," Cat's mom said.

"Outvoted, as usual," Daniel said.

Cat's mom turned to someone in a uniform and asked directions to their seats. She was as comfortable as if she were in her own home, and Jalen wondered if that was something she'd learned or if some people were just born that way.

Jalen choked with discomfort in the strange and fancy place, but when they walked through a doorway, then up some steps where the fading daylight washed over them along with the bright-white lights of the stadium, he seemed to be able to breathe again. The players were already out on the field, warming up. An usher directed them to the seats Jalen had been in on Sunday. Daniel's groan of joy barely registered as they sat. "Look at this! I died and went to heaven."

Jalen's eyes were on Yager, and it wasn't twenty seconds before he glanced over and gave Jalen a thumbs-up.

Jalen returned it and sat down between Daniel and Cat.

Daniel kept looking around. He nudged Jalen. "Can you believe this?"

"Yes," Jalen said.

"I can't."

Cat nudged Jalen. "Don't forget your glasses."

"Right," he said, putting them on. Even though it was getting dark, the glasses cut the glare from the lights and actually helped him see better.

A woman appeared with small menus and asked if they wanted anything. Cat's mom leaned forward and said to Daniel, "Pick out what you want, and we can order it later when you're hungry. Get whatever you want. It comes with the seats."

"What's that mean?" Daniel asked. "Like, it's free?"

"Yes," Cat's mom said. "Anyone want a drink?"

"Strawberry smoothie, please," Cat said.

"Yeah, make it two," Daniel said. "Please."

"Jalen?"

"Huh? No, I'm fine, but thank you."

Daniel leaned into him and whispered. "It's *free,* amigo. If you don't want one, order a blueberry for me."

"Blueberry," Jalen said, then turned his attention back to the field. He wanted to take it all in, not because he was savoring it, but because he wanted to make sure he was in the zone. Yager had to get a hit every time he got up, and Jalen had to be ready.

He focused on the action, willing time to slow down,

but it didn't. Before he knew it, the White Sox took the field but jogged off before Jalen had gotten a good look at Derek Holton's strange throwing motion. Everyone stood for the national anthem.

Masahiro Tanaka took the mound for the Yankees and didn't do Jalen any favors when he sat down the first three batters with just twelve pitches. The crowd roared its approval. Jalen watched Yankees manager Joe Girardi slap high fives with his team as they entered the dugout. Jalen caught Yager's eye as he went by, but they said nothing. Jalen might have been a stranger, and that made the whole thing seem like a dream. He realized he hadn't even tried to predict Tanaka's pitches and wondered if he should have.

The Yankees didn't help slow things down. Ellsbury and Gardner both got on before Reuben Hall grounded out. Jalen watched Holton carefully. He knew why they called him "the Condor." He looked like a giant bird. The thin, six-foot-six lefty had thrown ten pitches in all, and Jalen had only gotten a handle on the last three. Tegan Tollerson stepped up, and Jalen expected a changeup but saw it was a fastball and that flustered him, because he was rarely wrong . . . and this was no time to be wrong. Tollerson went down swinging as well, and Jalen's genius felt like a loosely screwed lightbulb, flickering on and off. The pressure and the excitement were messing with his brain.

Tyler Hutt went to the plate.

"Sinker," Jalen whispered under his breath.

It was a sinker, out of the strike zone, and Hutt passed on it.

"Slider." Jalen spoke without moving his lips. No one could hear him.

Holton threw his slider and Jalen breathed a sigh of relief. Hutt popped it over the second baseman's head for a single that scored the speedy Ellsbury and put runners on second and first. Yager moved to the on-deck circle, loaded his bat up with a doughnut, and began to swing as Joe Ros stepped up to the plate. Jalen wanted to watch the pitcher, but he couldn't keep his eyes off Yager.

Cat put a hand on Jalen's leg. "Jalen, you're shaking. Are you all right?"

Jalen felt his head shake the way you might flick away a housefly, because he wasn't all right. He was all wrong. He felt the urge to just get up and run. It was cowardly, he knew, but he couldn't help it, and it made him think of his mother.

She ran.

Somehow, he stayed put. He wasn't rewarded for his effort, though. Holton threw three pitches, and Jalen knew only one of them. Part of the reason might have been

Yager standing right there in front of him. Jalen tried to convince himself that was the problem and that he'd be fine when Yager got up.

It was a 1–2 count when a fastball came in that Jalen hadn't seen coming. Joe Ros reared back and blasted it. Jalen held his breath.

49

THE WHITE SOX RIGHT FIELDER LEAPED AT THE
wall and snagged Joe Ros's hit. The cheering crowd
deflated. The runners slowed and jogged back to the dugout. Ahead 1–0, but it should have been more. Yager held
his bat in what looked like a death grip. He gave Jalen a
grim look and returned to the dugout for his glove. The
White Sox had given Jalen some time, but that was all.
Yager would be up in the second inning no matter what
happened.

Jalen's skin felt too tight. He needed to move. He had to
get up. "Excuse me," he said.

"Are you okay?" Cat asked.

"Fine. I'll be right back." Jalen removed his sunglasses,

then slipped past them and up the stairs. He found his way back to the VIP Club buffet. Food was still piled high, but only a few people remained, eating and watching the game on one of several big screens. Everything was fancy and nice. Mirrors lined the walls, silver gleamed every-where. Jalen would have felt more at home on the moon. His eyes fell on the exit. His father had put a rumpled twenty-dollar bill into Jalen's pocket. He couldn't help thinking he could use it to take the subway and then a train back to Rockton.

Yager wasn't really going to have him arrested for stealing.

He knew that deep down. Too much time had passed.

"Can I get you something?" someone with a deep south-ern accent was asking.

Jalen turned. A big, thickset old man wearing a tall paper hat held a carving knife above a gently steaming prime rib.

"Uh, no," Jalen said. "I'm not hungry."

"Are you sick?" The man's kind eyes, like his skin, were the color of coffee, and tufts of cottony white hair peeked out from the edges of the hat band.

"No." Jalen was sick, but not in the way the man was asking.

"Already ate?" He smiled, revealing bright-white teeth.

"No."

"Piece of prime rib on one of these rolls with some dripping sauce might cheer you up. It's what I always loved about makin' food for folks." His voice reminded Jalen of distant thunder, low and gentle.

Jalen looked at the rolls. They were small and soft for making sliders. "They shouldn't have cut those. They dry out when you cut them."

The man squinted at the rolls. "Exactly what I said! How do you know about rolls?"

"My dad is a cook. I help in his restaurant. For about another week anyway." Jalen knew he sounded glum, and he wanted to explain. "Until the bank takes it."

The man chuckled and smiled warmly at him. "Well, there's always someone with problems worse than yours. Don't ever forget that."

"Like what?" The question popped out. Jalen glared and wondered how a complete stranger could have read him so easily.

The man's eyes sparkled, then dimmed. He got a faraway look, and his mouth fell. "Like me . . . lost my restaurant too. Rib shack. Not enough insurance. Whoever hears about fires anymore? Then I lost my wife." The man sighed. "*And* my little girl."

He began to shave some meat off the roast with his

carving knife, catching the pink slice on the bottom half of a roll. "Now I serve the food other people cook, and they don't have the sense to know you shouldn't cut rolls until you're ready to eat 'em."

The man's grumpy frown faded. His eyes brightened again and he smiled as he handed Jalen the sandwich. "Try this anyway. You don't usually get everything the way you want it, but if you stop enjoying the good things you do get, you've got no more sense than a pickle."

Jalen took the sandwich and bit into it to be polite. The prime rib melted in his mouth, filling it with delicious juices that made him take another bite.

"Fought that fire with a garden hose," the man said, "hoping for the trucks to get there in time. See, if you do everything you can, it lets you sleep at night, no matter how things turn out. Some things are bigger than we are. A lot of things, it turns out."

Jalen blinked at the man, wondering if he knew about Jalen the way Jalen knew about pitches, that he had some instinct that told him Jalen was on the verge of quitting.

Jalen took a deep breath and let it out slow.

The old man studied him and smiled. "I'll be here all the way up until nine if you find you'd like another of those."

"Thank you, Mr. . . ."

The man smiled. "Moses, but no mister stuff. People call me just Moses."

"Thank you, Mr. . . . Moses. I can't call you just Moses, Mr. Moses."

"Well, okay, but you eat that, then." Mr. Moses pointed with his carving knife.

Jalen tucked the rest of the slider in his mouth and wiped his fingers and lips on a napkin. He gave Moses a final salute and a smile, then returned to his seat.

"Tanaka's on fire." Daniel leaned across him to fist-bump Cat. "Another K, and Garcia grounded out."

Jalen fist-bumped Daniel as well, feeling better, feeling *excited*. He didn't know if it was the warm sandwich in his belly or the man's words in his head, but he knew he could do this. He wasn't going to look back one day and wonder. He wasn't going to run. He took out the sunglasses and put them on.

Ramírez punched a line drive into the 5-6 hole for a single, but Tanaka struck out Avila, ending the side. The Yankees jogged briskly to the dugout. Yager was still grim-faced, serious to the point of anger. He swapped out his glove for a bat and a helmet and quickly loaded the bat, taking a couple of swings as he watched Holton warming up.

Yager didn't look at Jalen until he rounded the plate

and stopped outside the batter's box for a last practice swing.

Jalen gave him a nod, then shifted his attention to Holton. He focused as hard as he could on the tall, birdlike pitcher, telling himself again that he could do this.

He felt Cat's hand on his arm. "Do you see it?" she whispered.

Jalen didn't reply, but he held up four fingers.

Yager saw him and stepped into the box.

Jalen clenched his teeth.

50

YAGER SWUNG FOR THE FENCES.

The ball popped up foul into the stands behind the visitor's dugout.

Yager crouched to retie his shoelace and snuck a glance at Jalen. Jalen flicked his eyes on the pitcher to be sure before holding up four fingers again. Yager's expression narrowed, as if in doubt, but he gave the slightest of nods and got into his stance.

Holton wound up and threw another four-seam fastball, but too far outside to swing. Jalen watched Holton wipe his thin red beard against his jersey and adjust his cap. He shook off the signal from the catcher. Jalen removed his glasses to make eye contact with Yager. Then he made a throat-cutting motion, because Holton was going after Yager with that nasty slider, a pitch that would break down and in on Yager, the toughest pitch for him to hit.

Jalen returned the glasses to his face. Yager took another practice swing, then a big, deep breath before stepping into the box.

"Jalen, you're hurting me." Cat pried his fingers off her knee.

"Sorry. It's that slider."

"Oh no," Cat said.

"What?" Daniel leaned into Jalen's face. "What's going on?"

"Just watch," Cat said.

Holton wound up and threw the slider. Yager swung and ripped it right over the pitcher's head. He took off for first. The center fielder played it on the bounce before tossing it to second base. JY was on, though. The crowd roared, and Jalen wondered if it was extra loud because of all the rumors that this was the end for the Yankees star who had helped deliver the 2009 World Championship to the hungry New York fans.

Jalen exhaled and sat back in his seat. Daniel pounded him on the back, and Cat kissed his cheek before clapping wildly. No one noticed, because the whole crowd was buzzing. Yager never looked back at Jalen from his spot on the first-base bag. It disappointed Jalen, but he reminded himself that he was there to do a job, and that job wasn't over. Yager would have two or maybe three more at bats, and he already knew Yager wasn't going to send the tweet that would save the Silver Liner unless he was a hundred percent.

The inning ended without a Yankees score. Jalen spent the next several innings studying and thinking about the Sox pitcher so hard that the three runs scored by the White Sox offense—two on a Todd Frazier homer—barely registered in his brain.

He could only think about Yager's next at bat.

When that chance finally came in the fifth, Jalen was trembling. He signaled fastball for the first pitch. The fastball came in low and inside. Yager swung and missed. Jalen watched and signaled for a second fastball. Yager swung early and pulled it foul. With an 0–2 count, Yager's face turned sour. His look seemed to blame Jalen.

Jalen ignored that. He studied the pitcher and gave Yager two thumbs-up, the signal for a changeup—a pitch thrown like a fastball but traveling slow enough to disrupt a player's timing. It was a pitch Yager could slam *if* he knew it was coming, and—if he trusted in Jalen—he knew it now.

Holton wound up and threw.

In it came, slow and fat.

51

YAGER BLASTED IT FAIR DOWN THE LEFT FIELD line.

Every fan in the stadium jumped up and cheered as Yager made it safely to second.

Didi Gregorius advanced him to third with a sacrifice before Ellsbury knocked the aging star in, making the score Yankees 2, White Sox 3 and bringing the crowd to its feet again. Even though Holton began to weaken after that, he got out of the fifth and sixth innings without another run.

When Holton threw three wild pitches in a row and walked Yager in the seventh with one out and a 3–2 lead, the White Sox pulled their ace and sent Zach Duke to the hill, and Jalen had to reset his mind.

"What's it mean?" Daniel asked.

Jalen chewed his lip. "A lot of nasty action. This guy's a sidearmed lefty who gave up his fastball about eight years ago."

Looking up his stats on her iPhone, Cat chimed in, "He used to be a starting pitcher. He was okay, but as a relief pitcher, he's money. Lefties against him are below .200, and righties don't do much better."

They watched it come true as Duke sat the last two batters in the Yankees lineup with just nine pitches. Jalen called the final two correctly, a cutter and a sinker, but he worried about Yager getting a hit with the filthy pitches Duke was sending across the plate.

Then a ray of hope struck him. If Duke could shut down the next six batters, Yager would have had a perfect night. But Jalen couldn't count on that. Just one walk or hit meant Yager would have to get by Duke, and Jalen had no idea if JY could do that, even if he did know what pitch was coming.

It felt wrong to root against his team, but Jalen couldn't help it. He'd rather save his dad's restaurant than have the Yankees win a single game out of 162. Still, it made him quiet, and Daniel's groaning in the bottom of the eighth as Hall grounded out again annoyed him. He stayed silent, though.

"What's wrong?" Cat asked.

Jalen shrugged. "Nothing."

"I know you better than that," she said.

Daniel excused himself to use the restroom. Cat gave Jalen a poke in the arm.

Jalen sighed and admitted to her that he hoped Yager wouldn't get up again, even though it meant the Yankees would lose.

Cat nodded. "I get it, but you're wrong."

"I know. It's awful. Who roots against his own team?"

"No, not because you're rooting against the Yankees," she said. "You're wrong because you can *do* this. I know you can. Stop doubting."

"You're right," Jalen said, then told her the story about Mr. Moses, the server in the VIP Club dining room who'd used a garden hose to try to stop a fire.

"That's right," Cat said. "Even if it doesn't work—which it will—you have to do everything you possibly can. That's all you can ever do, Jalen."

Daniel returned and sat down, out of breath. "I hurried back," he explained. "When I'm watching, it counts. I was watching the game last week on TV with my dad, and I went out of the room for five minutes to make a sandwich. In that time the Yanks had *two* errors, the Orioles scored three runs, and the Yankees lost 5–4."

"What does that even prove?" Cat wrinkled her face.

"Proves when I'm rooting, that wouldn't have happened." Daniel ignored her and turned his attention to the field, as if he'd just recited some gospel.

Bryan Mitchell had taken over on the Yankees mound for Tanaka in the seventh and had a good run shutting down the White Sox through the eighth. When he gave up a walk, a single, and another walk, loading the bases with just one out, Girardi came out of the dugout, walked to the mound, and took the ball, signaling for Dellin Betances. The sleepy crowd came to life.

For a few moments, Jalen forgot his problems, lost in the wonder and excitement of Betances's fastball and curve mix. The White Sox players swung and missed, swung and missed. With the third strikeout, the roar was deafening. Daniel jumped up and spilled his smoothie all over the wall in front of them. The four of them— even Cat's mom—high-fived one another and everyone around them.

The Yankees dashed into the dugout, ready for a last-inning rally.

Jalen knew what it meant. If they got their rally, and even a single runner got on, he and Yager would be put to the test. But instead of feeling nervous, Jalen was *excited*. He wanted to be a big-league player himself one day and maybe help win a game like this. Night had closed in around the packed stadium, and the glow of the lights holding back the black, empty sky made it feel like they could all be the last people on the planet, captured in a bubble of time and space where nothing else mattered.

What had Jeter told him?

Have fun.

Jalen shivered with the thrill of knowing that *he* might have a hand in a big-league win. If he did, and Yager was in the spotlight, batting four-for-four and saving the game, how much better would that make Yager's tweet? What bank would dare shut down Fabio DeLuca's Silver Liner Diner after it won a game for the Bronx Bombers?

In that moment Jalen wished he could help not just James Yager, but the entire team. What could Tollerson, Hutt, and Joe Ros do if *they* knew what pitches a Robertson was about to throw? He cleared his mind of that thought, though. That was for another day. Now he had to hope and pray that one of the three Yankee players batting before Yager could get on base.

That was all he and the Yankees needed.

52

TYLER HUTT DID IT.

With a 3–2 count, he jacked one deep into right field, where a fielding error turned a double into a triple.

Duke squinted at the tying run on third, then shook it off and sat Joe Ros before looking at James Yager the way a cat counts canaries. Despite a good night, Yager's recent batting average said his time had passed, and Duke was in his prime as a closer.

The crowd jumped to its feet, and waves of cheering rolled down onto the field. Yager looked back at the first row of seats, not at Jalen, but at Cat and her mom, giving them a wink. He marched to the plate, took two swings, and looked Jalen's way.

Jalen gave the signal for a fastball.

Yager stepped up. In came the fastball. Yager nicked it foul into the backstop and stepped back.

Jalen watched Duke, knowing he was going to throw another fastball but wanting to be sure. He signaled four fingers, and Yager stepped up. This time he whiffed, and the crowd felt it. The roar dulled, but then rebounded and grew again, this time hopeful.

Duke fought back a grin at the 0–2 count. He was noticeably confident that he could get out of the jam. Too disrespectful after Yager's recent slide.

Jalen's gut tightened. Everything said sinker, but Duke almost never threw his sinker. The percentage of sinkers he threw was in the single digits. It *couldn't* be a sinker, but it *was*. Jalen just knew it, and he gave the thumbs-down. Yager stepped toward the plate but froze midstep and backed away, signaling the umpire that he needed another moment. The ump glared, then after a moment called him up. Yager stared hard at Jalen.

"Let's go!" shouted the ump.

Jalen shook from the inside out but signaled thumbs-down again and pushed his hand toward Yager with a short, hard nod. Yager closed his eyes briefly, took a deep breath, and stepped into the box.

Duke wound up.

In it came.

Yager took an uppercut swing for the fences.

53

YAGER HIT IT ON THE SWEET SPOT.

It was a moon shot, Yager's first that season, a big, long, game-winning home run.

The crowd lost its mind.

Cat and her mom lost their minds.

Daniel lost his mind.

Jalen lost his breath and a buzz filled his brain. He was floating.

And then something happened that no one expected. Yager crossed home plate under the thunder of applause and waded through the backslapping mayhem of his teammates, only to appear at the wall, reach over, and hug Jalen DeLuca like his long-lost little brother.

It was a mistake they'd all soon regret.

54

YAGER BLURTED OUT THAT HE'D MEET THEM AT the diner, then disappeared into the Yankees dugout with the jubilant team. Jalen and his friends grinned at one another and chattered with excitement, standing at their seats as they waited for the crowd above them to clear.

"Excuse me!"

Jalen turned and saw a young blond woman with a microphone and a cameraman in tow. He froze.

"Hi!" The woman was at the wall now, pretty and bubbly and shoving the microphone in front of Jalen. "Wow, some win, huh? And that hug JY gave you . . . what was that all about?"

"Uh . . ." Jalen had no idea what to say. He looked at Cat

for help, but she was frozen too. Jalen thought maybe the woman would go away if he said nothing, but that didn't happen.

"Do you know JY?" she asked, pushing.

"Yes."

"A nephew or a cousin or something?" the reporter asked.

"I . . . I help him." The moment he said it, Jalen knew it was wrong, not wrong factually, but the wrong thing to say with a TV camera pointed at you.

Cat stepped in. "Jalen is JY's lucky charm. Really, it's the food at his dad's diner that did it."

"The . . . food?" The reporter looked to Cat's mom for signs of a joke but saw none. "So, tell me more."

Jalen felt relieved. Cat had saved him. He knew how mad Yager would be if Jalen blabbed about being a base-ball genius. Yager had told him specifically that he didn't want the GM or Yankees' owner to think his comeback was a trick. Jalen wasn't sure how he felt about that, being considered a trick, but things were going too well to mess them up with some reporter.

"Yeah, uh, my dad has a diner." Jalen's tongue twisted up. There was so much to say.

Cat leaned over to speak into the microphone. "Not just any diner. The Silver Liner Diner in Rockton, New York.

And it wasn't just any food. JY's lucky meal was the stuffed calamari that comes from Jalen's grandma back in Italy. Yager eats the lucky squid, and he goes four-for-four."

This caught the reporter's attention, and she shifted it to Cat. "Wait, how do you know Yager?"

"He's our next-door neighbor." Cat grinned up at her mom. "He came to my birthday party last week. Everyone knows he's been in a slump, but that's over now. You'll see. He's gonna tweet about it tonight. It'll be hard to get a seat in the Silver Liner after this."

The woman reporter looked at her watch, then the cameraman. "If we feed this now, we could get it on the end of the ten o'clock news and scoop everyone. Thanks, kids. Let's go."

"Wow," Daniel said. "What just happened?"

"Let the media frenzy begin." Cat beamed.

"I don't know," Jalen said.

"You don't know what?" Cat raised her eyebrows at him.

Jalen watched the reporter disappear from the field. "I just got a feeling Yager's not going to be very happy about it."

55

JALEN FELL ASLEEP ON THE RIDE HOME.

The day had done him in, and the joy of success and a dramatic Yankees win with him and Yager at the center of it all left him exhausted. When Cat's mom slowed the Range Rover to exit the highway, he woke and looked around, blinking.

Cat twisted around from her front seat and held her phone in his face. "I didn't want to wake you, but look. He did it. Right after the game."

On the screen was one of the pictures Cat had taken of Yager with a big smile to go with his delicious-looking plate of calamari. Yager himself had tweeted:

SLUMP OVER THX 2 #SILVERLINERDINER
IN ROCKTON. #LUCKYCALAMARI
HELPED ME GO 4 FOR 4!

A jolt of excitement lit Jalen from the inside out. "Wow. He really did."

"He said he would." Cat grinned all around. "A deal's a deal. Next stop, a contract."

"Not yet." Jalen scowled. Reality came crashing in on him. "I've got to do it again tomorrow night and Friday, too."

"You will!" Cat grabbed his knee and shook it. "You proved you can do it, and you'll do it again. It's as good as done, Jalen. Why the face?"

Jalen looked at Daniel to see if he knew.

Daniel pressed his lips tight, then said, "The whole reason for all of this was so Jalen could play with the Rockets, not get a contract with Yager."

"Yeah, but he can do both!" Cat's face glowed with delight. "This is really happening!"

Daniel wagged his head. "He can't do both unless someone gets Coach Gamble on board. Jalen can't even be late again if he wants to stay on the team. He sure can't miss a practice."

"It's true." Jalen opened the window to get some air

and had a fuzzy recollection of a story from his early childhood his dad would tell. "Gamble is the ogre under the bridge. I'm the goat."

"It was a troll," Cat said. "'Three Billy Goats Gruff.' And the goats outsmarted him."

Cat's mom cleared her throat. "What if James Yager spoke to him?"

Jalen froze. His mind whirred with the possibilities. "He'd do that?"

"Why wouldn't he?" Cat's mom said.

"Ha-ha! See?" Cat clapped her hands and patted her mom's shoulder.

Just then they rounded the corner in the center of town.

"What's that?" Daniel pointed up ahead.

In the white glow behind the train station, half a dozen red lights flashed madly, illuminating everything in a frantic, hellish glow. The Range Rover slowed, circling the station and crossing the tracks. Several spotlights lit the Silver Liner. Fire trucks and emergency vehicles surrounded it. A frenzy of firefighters glowed like aliens in their yellow coats and wide hats.

Smoke and steam drifted up from the diner into the blackest of nights.

56

IT WAS LIKE THE END OF THE WORLD.

The end of everything.

The lights were out and the diner was like a crow-eaten carcass, lifeless and empty. The damp, sickly scent of smoke filled their noses even inside the car. Cat let loose a small shriek.

"Dad!" Jalen screamed, and launched himself from the SUV.

He'd nearly reached the front of the diner when a fire-fighter swept him up and carried him back toward the trucks. "Oh, no. You can't go in there."

Jalen kicked and flailed. "My dad! Where's my dad?"

Another firefighter caught hold of him as well, and

together they pinned Jalen down on the bumper of the fire engine. Jalen suddenly went limp. Before him was the back end of an ambulance. A paramedic slammed the doors shut and ran around to the front of the ambulance.

Before Jalen could speak, it was gone.

57

JALEN CLOSED HIS EYES, THINKING THE WORST.
The cook's words from the ballpark haunted him. Things
could always be worse. And a restaurant fire just like what
happened to Mr. Moses? The whole thing felt to Jalen like
some horrible and impossible dream.

Then he heard his name.

"Jalen! Jalen!"

Jalen opened his eyes and saw his father's beautiful
red face. Sweat gleamed on his bald head and his upper
lip, and the edges of his glasses were foggy.

The firefighters let go and his father hugged him. Jalen
was shaking, and he realized his face was damp with
tears. "Dad, you're all right?"

"I'm all right." His father held him at arm's length. "Nobody is hurt. Just the diner."

His dad looked and sighed, shaking his head. "I sent Greta and Jimmy home and then people started coming. They talked about the Yankees and James Yager and they wanted the lucky calamari. So I started to cook and I saw more people coming, and I tried to cook more calamari, and I left the stove 'cause I don't want people to think I wasn't there, and then a man he showed me you on the news and I watched, but then I went back to the stove and . . ."

"Me on the news." Jalen's voice fell flat, and he looked at the smoking diner. "How bad is it, Dad?"

His father turned and looked with him, keeping one arm around Jalen's shoulders. "I dunno. Maybe it's not so bad. I gotta get a new stove. That much is for sure."

Jalen suddenly panicked. "Do we have insurance?"

"Yes, yes," his father said. "Don't you worry. I have insurance."

"But now people will come and they won't be able to eat." Jalen was thinking of the bank even as his friends surrounded him.

Cat's mom looked sadly at the diner. "Maybe we can help."

"Everyone can help!" Cat said.

Jalen looked at Cat, because she didn't sound sad, she sounded happy and excited.

"We can turn this into a whole community thing." Cat waved her arms. "We can get James Yager and the town— maybe even my cheapskate stepfather will kick in."

"Maybe the Yankees?" Daniel suggested.

"Yes!" Cat pumped a fist. "The Yankees will want to help. They always do stuff like that. Everyone will, and it'll be an even bigger story and it'll be even *better!* We can have a grand reopening! Everyone will want to be a part of it."

Jalen felt a bubble of excitement building in his chest, only to feel it pop. He didn't want it to pop, but it did because he was certain about one thing.

"No, Cat," he said. "Not everyone."

58

BEFORE JALEN COULD GO INTO DETAIL, JAMES
Yager appeared, looking exhausted and worried.

After Cat's mom explained everything, he put a hand on Jalen's dad's shoulder. "I'm sorry, Fabio. I'd be happy to help."

Jalen brightened. "Thank you."

"Well, you're helping me, right?" Yager looked at him hard. "We have to help each other."

Jalen opened his mouth to bring up the subject of Coach Gamble, but his father spoke.

"Thank you. It'll be okay." Jalen's dad forced a smile. "It'll be like a phoenix, the bird that rises from the ashes."

"I hope so." Yager stared at the diner for a minute.

"Well, I gotta get some rest. Victoria, you set it up with the kids. The tickets will be at the window. Same thing tomorrow, right?"

Everyone nodded. Jalen opened his mouth for the second time to raise the subject of Coach Gamble, but two firefighters broke into their party, thrilled to recognize JY in their midst. Firefighters began to line up to take selfies, and Yager obliged, forcing tired smiles.

The fire marshal took Jalen's dad aside to try to explain what he'd need to do to make the diner safe before he could open again. Jalen tried to listen, knowing his dad didn't always totally understand, even though he'd always pretend he did. When they'd finished, Yager had gone, and Jalen knew he'd have to deal with Coach Gamble himself in the morning.

The trucks and Jalen's friends didn't disappear until after midnight. He and his dad walked home in silence. Before Jalen dropped into bed, his father said, "Everything's gonna be all right, Jalen. I got you and you got me. The rest? We'll see . . . we'll just see."

Jalen tossed and turned, but he must have slept through the four o'clock train. When the five o'clock train woke him, though, he knew he couldn't get back to sleep, so he went to the diner out of habit, walking the tracks in the faint morning light. From the back, he could see where the fire had burned through. The gaping hole exposed blackened ribs of wall studs, and the damp smell of smoky soot still clung to the air. He rounded the diner to the front, where broken windows smiled wickedly with jagged teeth of glass. A thick strand of yellow tape marked DANGER blocked the front door.

The newspaper lay on the stoop as it always did, and Jalen looked around for the delivery person, wondering why he bothered. He sat on the steps to read with his back to the ruin. There was nothing about Jalen or the diner in the paper, just a Yankees box score and the story of Yager's dramatic comeback to lead the team to victory. Jalen had that sense again that everything might have simply been a strange dream, and he wished more than ever for an iPhone or Internet at home so he could experience all the excitement on social media.

He returned home and had a bowl of cereal, waiting until he heard the sound of the shower before he used his father's old flip phone to call Coach Gamble.

"Hello?" Coach Gamble sounded awake but grumpy.

Jalen swallowed. "Uh, Coach?"

"Who is this?"

"Coach, it's Jalen DeLuca."

"Pretty early, isn't it?"

"I know. Sorry." Jalen took a breath and launched into

his story, explaining that James Yager had invited him again to the Yankees game, because last night Jalen had been a kind of lucky charm. He spoke fast but never mentioned what he'd really done to help. His words pattered down on the coach's ears like a rainstorm until, finally, he had nothing left to say.

He could hear Coach Gamble breathing, but he had to ask, "Coach, are you there?"

Coach Gamble snorted. "This doesn't even make sense," he said gruffly. "There's no such thing as luck. I think you've heard me say that. Listen, I told you, you can get your money back and we all move on. If you can't make it to practice tonight, that makes it easy."

"But Coach, I—"

"Listen, kid. You're making more of this than you should." Coach Gamble's voice turned soft but stayed firm. "You have no idea how hard it is to go to the next level. I mean, you're a natural athlete. You're fast, and you can jump, but even if you did train with us, baseball is about a lot more than being an athlete. A lot of it is mental. You should think about focusing on track. Maybe football."

Jalen heard the shower go off. He felt his whole future slipping away. He didn't care what Coach Gamble said. Jalen had a dream, and he believed he could make it come true. One thing he knew for certain: it wouldn't happen if he missed a summer of baseball. He'd never catch up.

"Listen, Coach," he blurted into the phone. "I shouldn't have called. I'll be there tonight. I can still be on the team if I'm there, right?"

"If you're there *on time*, yes." Coach Gamble bristled with impatience. "The rules are the rules. I don't go back on my rules, and you've got a spot on the team. Only you can end that, I already said."

"Okay, Coach. Sorry. See you tonight." Jalen hung up and put the phone down on the table where his father had left it.

"Jalen?" His father wandered in, wrapped in one towel and drying off with another. He sounded tired and sad. "How are you doing?"

Jalen tried to brighten his face with a smile. "I'm fine, Dad. Okay. How are *you*?"

"Is a sad day for me, Jalen." His father's eyes were red from either smoke or tears. "But who knows? Maybe everything is gonna be fine. We'll see. . . ."

59

JALEN GOT READY FOR SCHOOL. HE WAS AFRAID
to ask his dad for the phone to call Yager, and he decided
he'd let Cat send Yager a text informing him about the
baseball practice he had to be at unless . . .

Jalen kissed his dad good-bye and set his jaw as he
walked down the winding gravel path toward the bus
stop. Why should he take on the worry about Coach
Gamble? If anyone could get him to make an exception to
his almighty rules, it had to be James Yager. Jalen should
have had Yager ask in the first place.

When he rounded the bend to a spot where he could
see the diner, Jalen noticed a big white Ford F-350 pickup
truck parked right in front. As he got closer, he saw that

the tape had been cut. The truck had a large green decal on the door that said GCS. Jalen knew he had time before the bus, so he climbed the steps, listening. Inside, except for broken glass, the dining area didn't look so bad. There were some overturned chairs and two tables that needed to be cleared, but other than the smell, no one would have suspected a fire.

Something clanked in the kitchen.

Jalen crept toward the door, ready to jump, because he knew it swung both ways and whoever had the pickup truck might come through any second. When he heard the murmur of voices, he pushed through. The kitchen was a mess. Puddles still stood on the floor, and sunlight streamed through the big hole, exposing charred metal and wood. The stove looked like a bomb had gone off. Two men in dark-green caps with clipboards stared at him.

They both wore jeans and work boots. The shorter one had a long, bushy mustache. He scowled at Jalen with dark eyes. "Hey, kid, this is a work zone. You shouldn't be in here."

"I . . . it's my dad's place."

The man's face softened. "Oh. Well, we're here to help. When will he get here?"

"He . . . I don't know. Soon?"

"Well, we got orders to get this fixed up."

"Can you?"

The shorter man laughed, and the big one looked at Jalen curiously. "That's what we do. Our owner knows James Yager, you know, the Yankees second baseman?"

"Yes," Jalen said.

"Yeah, well, we got the word to get this place fixed up *fast*." The man nudged a burnt pan on the floor with his toe.

"How fast?" Jalen looked around at the mess. "I mean . . ."

The shorter man looked around too and chuckled. "Well, it's still here, so I don't know"—he looked at his partner—"a day or two?"

The big man nodded, and Jalen felt his heart leap. "Really? The stove?"

"We got stoves. Stoves are easy. We patch up this wall here, clean up the mess, get some fans going. Electrical will need rewiring. But kid"—the man smiled broadly—"we're Greenland Construction. We build practically every fast-food restaurant up and down the thruway. We got two hundred men in the Westchester office alone, and when our boss says get it done? Trust me, it'll get done."

Jalen was so excited, the diner getting repaired was all he talked about on the bus with Daniel. It wasn't until they pulled up to the school, where Cat stood waiting for them, that he remembered Coach Gamble.

"Hey, guys." Cat wore a serious look. She listened to

Jalen's story about the Greenland Construction people before she said, "That's great, but what about tonight? Did you talk to Coach Gamble? Are you all set?"

Jalen looked at Daniel, who only shrugged. Kylie Wines, a tall, thin girl with fiery red hair, saw Jalen and pulled up short. "Jalen! I saw you on the news. I saw JY's tweet. Everyone's talking. Will you take a selfie with me?"

Cat rolled her eyes. Jalen shrugged. "Sure."

Kylie took her picture, checked it, and jumped in the air before thanking Jalen and disappearing into the school. The rest of the kids streamed past the three of them, standing there in front of the entrance. Jalen noticed a few looks and pointed fingers, but no one else stopped for a photo.

"So," Cat said impatiently, "Coach Gamble? Are we set?"

"I don't know how to say this, exactly." Jalen raised his hands.

Cat scowled. "Just say it."

60

"COACH GAMBLE SAID NO. YOU HAVE TO TEXT
Yager. He's going to have to convince Coach Gamble."
Jalen started to move toward the school. "There, I said it."

Cat caught up to him. "Wait a minute, what do you
mean, he said no?"

"He said no, Cat. It doesn't get any simpler, and I'm *not*
going to get thrown off that team." It was somehow easier
for Jalen to speak as he walked. "That would defeat the
purpose of this whole thing."

"But you're a baseball genius." Cat kept her voice low
but filled with venom. "You could make a living doing this.
You could make *millions*."

"That's no joke." Daniel nodded in agreement, tagging

along like a pilot fish. "Last night was the bomb."

Jalen stopped short. "You know what my dad said to me last night? And he doesn't even know about the construction company. He said we've got each other, and that's all we need. Well, for me to be *me*, I have to play baseball. That's who I am. I don't care what anyone says. *I* say, and I'm not screwing that up for anything or anyone. Maybe I can do my genius thing for someone else, I don't know."

"Someone *else*?" Cat wrinkled her face. "After everything James Yager has done for you?"

Jalen grabbed the tight curly hair on his head. "This whole thing is a mess. Tweets and fires and GMs and contracts. I just want to play *baseball*, Cat."

He could see Cat didn't understand. She was looking at him like a bug she'd found floating in her drink, and it enraged Jalen.

"He's got a *game* to get ready for," she hissed. "How's he supposed to convince *your* coach to let you miss practice?"

"I don't know." Jalen turned to his locker and spun the dial. "He's James Yager. He'll figure it out."

"You can't dump this on him, Jalen." She grabbed him and spun him around.

"I'm dumping it on you." Jalen scowled. "You dump it on him."

"Why shouldn't *you* do it?" She narrowed her eyes in a mean way.

A small voice inside him told him to patiently explain to her that he didn't have a phone to text Yager with, but that should have been so obvious that it infuriated Jalen.

"Because he's not *my* future stepfather," Jalen blurted.

Cat flinched as if he'd snapped her with a belt. Her eyes filled.

Jalen felt his stomach climb into his throat. "I didn't mean that. Cat, I'm sorry." He reached for her arm, but he was too late.

Cat was gone.

61

DANIEL LOOKED AT JALEN SADLY.

"What?" Jalen demanded.

"You're acting like a real bad batch of hot sauce." Daniel turned to his locker and spun the combination. "*Extra* hot."

"What is 'hot sauce' anyway?" Jalen scowled. "Is it a curse word?"

"Hot sauce can be really good or really bad, amigo." Daniel slammed his locker shut. "And I bet you're smart enough to know this is the kind that keeps you running to the bathroom."

Jalen let him go, and when he walked into homeroom, he made sure he didn't even look Daniel's way.

The day wore on and Jalen paid little attention to his schoolwork. He took nearly a dozen more selfies with people in the halls, but his smiles were forced. He took no pleasure in his dash of fame. The one time he ran into Chris Gamble, his new teammate snorted. "Hey, it's the Calamari Kid!"

People around him laughed, and the name seemed to catch on. Jalen tried to ignore it.

At lunch he sat down by himself, but Daniel found him and sat without speaking. Jalen tried hard to ignore the sight of Cat sitting with Chris Gamble and Dirk Benning and their gang, but it made it difficult for him to eat.

Finally Daniel spoke. "Famous or not, you know, you gotta apologize."

"I'm sorry," Jalen said sharply.

"Not to me, and not like that."

Jalen sighed. "I am sorry, Daniel. You know I'm not famous. I feel like I'm losing my mind. You understand about being a baseball player, right?"

"Bro, we always said we'd play in the big leagues *together*. I know what you mean."

"And I can't not play this summer, right? If I miss a whole summer on the big field, I'll never catch up, right?"

Daniel crumpled the wrappings of his lunch into his brown bag. "Ninety feet seems like forever."

"And the Rockets are the only show in town," Jalen said.

"For anyone chasing the big show, it is." Daniel nodded.

"So I can't miss tonight," Jalen said. "Maybe Yager will go four-for-four without me? He won't have to face Holton. That's one good thing."

"Maybe he'll convince Coach Gamble to let you go," Daniel said.

"How's he gonna do that?"

Daniel shrugged. "He's James Yager."

62

AFTER THE LAST PERIOD, JALEN WAS STUFFING
books in his locker when he felt a tap on his shoulder.
He was surprised to see Cat. She looked prettier than
ever. Her blue eyes were on fire and a flush painted her
cheeks.

She held out her iPhone. "It's on. We'll pick you up at
the same time in front of the diner."

Jalen squinted at the phone. "What's that?"

"A text chain between me and JY," she said. "You need
to see it?"

"Coach Gamble's okay? I'm not gonna lose my spot?"
Jalen scowled. "That's hard to believe."

"So call him yourself." Cat held out the phone.

Emotions flooded Jalen. He tried to keep his hand from shaking as he took the phone from her. He blinked and brought Coach Gamble's number up in his mind, dialed it, and waited.

"Hello?" The coach sounded his usual grumpy self.

"Coach? It's Jalen DeLuca. I just wanted to make sure you're okay with me missing practice tonight."

"I said I was, didn't I?" Coach Gamble sounded annoyed. "I don't say what I don't mean. Bus leaves at six a.m. Saturday for the tournament. Don't be late for that. You miss that, you're gone. Anything else?"

"No, Coach."

"Good, because I got a day job here." The coach hung up abruptly.

Jalen handed the phone back and whispered, "Thank you, Cat."

"Hey, what are friends for?" Her voice was too cold for her words.

Jalen looked into her empty eyes and practically choked. "Well, I mean . . . you know I feel the same way about you."

Cat's eyes matched her voice. "I'm not talking about you, Jalen. I'm talking about James Yager. I did it because he's my friend. By the way, James gave Coach Gamble a check from his foundation for your four-hundred-ninety-dollar fee. In case you were worried about him keeping his word."

Cat turned and walked away, speaking as she went. "Pick you up at five."

63

TREES EXPLODED WITH FRESH GREEN BUDS, AND
the brilliant spring sunshine bathed the clapboard-and-
brick homes of Rockton. Jalen said good-bye to Daniel
when the bus stopped at his corner in the center of
town.

"I wish you were coming tonight." Jalen bumped
Daniel's fist.

"Yeah, but I'm not the baseball genius," Daniel said.
"Just do your thing, and then I can be there tomorrow
night for the final chapter in the salvation of James Yager.
That'll be something."

"If it happens."

"Why wouldn't it? You gotta think positive," Daniel said.

In Jalen's mind were banks and fires, construction workers, reporters, and the Yankees GM, but he only said, "Yeah, you're right."

He got off the bus and headed for home. When he turned the corner by the train station, he got a surprise.

64

THE SILVER LINER PARKING LOT OVERFLOWED
with trucks, and the diner itself boiled with men in
yellow hard hats. A crane had taken up a position in
the back, and Jalen watched in amazement as it lowered an enormous stove into a hole in the roof. A huge
tractor trailer hissed and groaned, easing out of the lot
and across the tracks. The truck spewed thick diesel
smoke as it passed Jalen, hauling a container filled with
charred debris.

The sounds of power tools, generators, and pounding
hammers filled the air with a delightful symphony of work.

Just in front of the steps to the diner, Jalen's father stood
looking over some plans with the shorter construction guy

Jalen had seen that morning. A yellow hard hat covered his bald head, but his cheeks were aglow.

"Jalen!" His father hugged him tight, then let him go and pointed. "Look! Look! I cannot believe all this. Joe here, he's a miracle worker. Can you believe?"

"No." Jalen shook his head. "It's amazing."

"And all because of Mr. Yager." Jalen's dad beamed. "Jalen, he called this morning, and you know what he said?"

"No."

"He asked me if can I make *nonna*'s calamari. He wanted it for luck, and I made it at home, and he came by. You just missed him!" Jalen's dad hugged him again. "He gonna tweet about the calamari tonight and he gonna tweet tomorrow night, and then on the Saturday, we gonna have a party and celebrate him and the Yankees, and the Silver Liner, she's gonna be open again!"

His father began to laugh, and Joe couldn't help a smile breaking out below his mustache.

Suddenly his father stopped, and his eyebrows met. "Jalen, what's the matter? You look like you ate a bad fish."

Jalen shook his head. It was too much to explain. He was happy, but it was buried under so much other stuff that he felt as though he were being smothered.

"You gotta rest is what." His father spoke softly. "Come on. I take-a you home. You get a nap, then I feed you, then you go make-a the miracles. Joe, I be right back."

"I got it, Fabio." Joe rolled the plans into a tube and tapped the side of his head. "You take your time."

Jalen let his father put an arm around him and guide him down the gravel path toward home. His father was right. Jalen was exhausted, and it took an effort just to lift his legs. They got home, and he lay down on his bed.

"I take-a you shoes off." His father spoke quietly, reaching for Jalen's feet. "You close-a the eyes."

Jalen did, and he took deep breaths as his shoes came off. Even the steady, muted sound of construction wasn't enough to keep him from dozing off.

65

JALEN WOKE WITH A START. HIS EYES POPPED
open and he looked around his room, figuring out
where he was and what was happening. He had just
one clear moment before an avalanche of thoughts and
emotions tumbled through his brain. He felt heavy still,
but rested, and the smells of red sauce and calamari
filled his nose.

"Dad?"

"Jalen! You sleep a good sleep, and now I got the
calamari for you." His father's voice floated in from the
kitchen. "Come eat!"

Jalen washed his hands and sat down at the table.

His dad set a plate of steaming food in front of him with

a fork, knife, and napkin. "I make it for Mr. Yager, but I save some for you and me."

"Nice, Dad. Thanks." Jalen dug in, and the food along with his nap raised his spirits. The steady sound of construction helped as well.

His father sat with a plate of his own, and they ate in silence. After they'd cleaned up, Jalen changed into a Yankees T-shirt, and they walked to the diner.

"He's like an angel, Mr. Yager, no?" his father said as the busy diner came into view.

"He is." Jalen thought about how close he'd come to ruining everything for his own selfish reasons. He swept the guilt aside, though, because everything was going perfectly. It was as if the whole thing had been written down before and they were simply following the script.

Jalen's dad gave him a hug and a kiss before putting on his hard hat and disappearing into the diner. Jalen wormed his way through the trucks, heading for the station, where it would be easier for Cat's mom to pick him up. He found an empty bench where he could see the street and took it.

Rays of sunlight splashed against the buildings and signs in town. A breeze swished through the trees, sweeping clean the sound of hammers and saws. It was dreamlike, just sitting there by himself in the warm sun with everything going his way.

The Range Rover turned the corner with the glare on its windshield winking.

Jalen took a deep breath and couldn't help smiling. He felt even his tiff with Cat was something that was meant to fade away with ease, and despite their quarrel, he opened the back door with a confident smile of having the dream come true.

The face staring at him from the backseat was the stuff of nightmares.

66

CHRIS GAMBLE'S FACE SEEMED TO GLISTEN WITH sweat beneath the Yankees cap he wore at an angle. His eyes widened with pleasure at the sight of Jalen's dismay, and he snorted a laugh.

"Hey, it's the Calamari Kid!" Chris said. "Happy birthday!"

Jalen looked into the front seat, because he couldn't believe this was really happening. Cat's mom looked back at Jalen with something that might have been pity, but Cat sat staring straight ahead without comment.

"You know Chris, right, Jalen?" Cat's mom asked.

"What's happy birthday?" Jalen asked Chris.

"I hate to brag, but you must feel like you got a present or something, getting to miss practice and go to the Yankees game with a future Hall of Famer." Chris stuck a fat thumb into his own chest. Jalen winced at the smell of his breath. It smelled like onions and dog food from a can.

"Then don't," Jalen said flatly.

"Don't what?" Chris asked.

"Brag." Jalen put his seat belt on and turned toward the window.

Chris chuckled softly to himself and uttered what might have been "mutt" under his breath. Jalen could only guess what had gone wrong, because Cat didn't seem to be talking to him, and he couldn't just blurt out, *What the heck is this jerk doing here?* to Cat's mom.

It wasn't hard to figure out, either. When Yager talked to Coach Gamble, he must have either offered to bring Chris as part of the deal, or Chris's dad squeezed it out of him in exchange for allowing Jalen to miss practice. Normally you wouldn't think of anyone squeezing anything out of James Yager, but Coach Gamble was far from normal.

"He couldn't have offered World Series tickets or something? A signed bat? His Cy Young trophy? Anything but *this*," Jalen grumbled to himself.

Jalen felt a huff of air against his cheek. The smell made him want to gag.

Chris was blowing his bad breath directly at Jalen and grinning at Jalen's discomfort. He was as disgusting as he was big and ugly. Jalen was angrier at Cat than he was at

Chris. She should have known better. Even if Cat was mad, she had to know having Chris with them would not only be a distraction to Jalen while he was doing his thing, but it could be dangerous. If Chris noticed something going on between Jalen and Yager, they could count on him not keeping it a secret.

Well, Jalen told himself, cracking the window for some fresh air, that was Yager's problem. All Jalen had to do was call the pitches.

By the time they got to the stadium, Jalen was in a better frame of mind. The atmosphere was like a carnival, with people milling outside the stadium, most of them wearing Yankees gear and soaking up the warm spring evening. Chris slouched along beside Cat, his hulking figure cutting a natural path through the crowd. Jalen tucked in behind Cat's mom, staying far from Cat and trying his best to ignore her as hard as she was ignoring him.

This time they went through security, got their tickets, and rode the elevator to the VIP Club with no problem. Jalen looked for Mr. Moses, who he'd spoken to the night before, but saw no sign of him. He kept quiet as they moved through the club toward the seats.

"Hey, how about we eat some of this grub?" Chris pulled up short in front of a roast turkey carving station. "Looks like it's free."

Cat's mom consulted her watch. "Uh, yes. We can."

"If it's okay, I'll just go to the seats," Jalen said.

Cat's mom hesitated, but then agreed that would be fine. Jalen left them, happy to be by himself and marveling at how quickly things had changed. Last night he and Cat and Daniel were on an adventure together, like the three musketeers. Tonight it was all about business, and the bitterness in the air stung Jalen's feelings. Still, the night was warm and the players' uniforms glowed beneath the lights. The grass looked freshly cut, and the dirt was lined to perfection.

Jalen found their seats and took the last one, closest to the Yankees dugout. He watched Yager warming up with his teammates and gave him a small wave when the second baseman looked his way. Yager tilted his head and shrugged, probably because he didn't expect Jalen to be alone.

The Yankees soon finished their warm-ups, and the White Sox took the field. Quintana had the mound, and Jalen put his sunglasses on and studied him carefully, eager to get a feel for things before Chris showed up. He shut his eyes briefly, and the numbers for the pitcher lit up his brain. All there, the improved ERA, the uptick in his changeup, the mile an hour he'd added to his fastball velocity, cutter, and curve. Jalen smiled to himself and opened his eyes only to realize someone had come and sat down next to him, and it wasn't Cat, her mom, or Chris.

67

JEFFREY FOXX DIDN'T LOOK AT JALEN, BUT HE PUT an arm around the back of Jalen's seat like an old friend. He wore a dark-navy pinstripe suit with a blue bow tie, and Jalen felt the tension coming off him like the heat off a hot bun. Foxx was chewing gum that left a hint of cinnamon in the air, but his mouth moved almost without effort.

"Saw you on the news last night." The GM let the words hang out there.

Jalen didn't know how to reply, but the longer the silence grew, the more he felt like he had to speak. He was thankful for the sunglasses to hide behind.

"Yeah," he said. "It was a nice win."

Foxx nodded slowly. "Reminded me of the James Yager I met when I took this club over five years ago."

Silence again until Jalen finally broke it. "He had a good night."

Now the GM looked directly at Jalen with an impish smile. "Well, he had that lucky calamari, right?"

Jalen shrugged. "Yeah, you know how players are. Superstitious."

"I do know." Foxx folded his arms across his chest now, wrinkling his suit as well as his face. "In fact, that's why I'm good at this management thing. In a world of lucky rabbits' feet, chicken dinners, backward rally caps, and now—apparently—calamari, I'm still all about numbers. That's why they use the *G* word when they talk about me—*genius*. Most people don't get numbers past two plus two, but me? I can see numbers in my mind like big billboards of graphs and formulas and endless statistics."

Foxx reached over, raised the sunglasses, and locked eyes with Jalen. "I don't expect you to understand, but do you have any idea what the odds are of James Yager going four-for-four three games in a row?"

Jalen knew the odds exactly—3,547,062 to 1—based on a sample group of statistics from last season in his brain, but all he did was shrug.

"It can't happen." The GM shook his head. "Not in the

world of numbers. It's odds, and you can't beat odds. They always win out. Look at Las Vegas. Just odds. But they've stripped people of enough money to build a jeweled city in the desert.

"Anyway." Foxx let Jalen's glasses drop into place, then slapped Jalen's knee gently before standing up. "I got my eye on you. Why? Because there's something going on. . . . I have no idea what, but there's no such thing as coincidence. I won't even mention lucky calamari."

With a wink, the GM slipped over the wall and disappeared into the dugout.

68

CAT'S MOM APPEARED, WITH CAT AND CHRIS
behind her. "Who was that, Jalen?"

"Just Jeffrey Foxx. He's the GM," Jalen said. "I met him when I came to the stadium the other day."

Cat's mom sat down next to Jalen. Cat sat as far from Jalen as she could, with Chris between her and her mom. Jalen tried to ignore that and focus on the field. He had a job to do, and it made him nervous to know Foxx might be watching. He so wanted to ask Cat what she thought, but with Cat's mom and Chris between them, she might have been a million miles away.

CC Sabathia had the mound for the Yankees, but he started out slow, letting two batters on before ending the top of the first. As Yager passed Jalen on his way into the dugout, he gave him a grin, showing no signs of knowing anything about the GM. Jalen couldn't smile back, even though he tried.

Jalen watched Quintana climb the mound. He had the baby face of a boy, but he looked big enough to be a linebacker, and his pitching was nasty. Jalen thought about Holton and Quintana, excellent pitchers surrounded by a team that struggled to score runs. Jalen knew you had to be at the right place at the right time, in sports and in life, too. On the Yankees, the two of them might be superstars. That made him think of his own team, and he looked over at Chris. He was having a laugh with Cat.

"Right time and place for him," Jalen muttered under his breath.

"What's that, Jalen?" Cat's mom asked.

"Where do you think the GM watches the game from?"

"Probably up there." She pointed across the stadium at the upper tier. "That's where the owner's box is. I imagine the GM is either there or somewhere close."

"How . . . how do you know?" Jalen couldn't help asking as Ellsbury approached the plate to start the Yankees off.

"Oh, my husband." She waved her hand to show she wasn't impressed. "We came one night for a fund-raiser."

"In the owner's box?" Jalen asked.

"Yes. The governor was there too," she said with a yawn. "And the mayor. Anyway, that's where it is."

Jalen glanced up where she was pointing and the glint of something like a mirror caught his eye, but the crowd came to life at the sight of Ellsbury. Jalen had a job to do. He focused on Quintana.

The pitcher was red hot. He sat the first three Yankee batters, and the White Sox charged their dugout, slapping Quintana high fives. During the measly eleven throws it took to end the inning, Jalen hadn't been able to predict a single pitch.

The second inning began with CC giving up a single but striking out one batter before Yager snagged a wicked line drive, leaping, catching it, and delivering a rocket to first base, surprising the runner as well as the crowd. Yager tipped his hat on the way to the dugout. Jalen felt a flicker of joy, but the muddle of not being able to read the pitcher weighed him down.

In the bottom of the second, Tegan Tollerson got things going with a double on the second pitch. Hutt struck out in four, and then Joe Ros knocked one in the 5-6 hole on his first pitch, putting runners on first and third. Quintana had thrown a total of eighteen pitches.

Yager was up. He glanced at Jalen as he left the on-deck circle. Jalen didn't blink. Yager rounded the plate, took his warm-up swings, then looked directly at Jalen.

Jalen ground his teeth.

He looked at the pitcher so hard his eyes hurt.

"Let's go," the ump barked. "Batter up!"

Yager stepped into the box, staring hard at Jalen.

Jalen could only shake his head.

He had no idea what Quintana was going to throw.

69

THE WHITE SOX PITCHER THREW A CURVEBALL

that nicked the outside of the plate. Yager let it go for a strike. He stepped out of the box, and his eyes went immediately to Jalen, who could only shake his head and hold up his hands. In his mind, he saw the construction crews pulling out of the Silver Liner's parking lot, leaving it with the repairs only partially complete.

From the corner of his eye, Jalen caught Cat looking at him. He turned his head just enough to see Chris staring as well. Jalen fought back tears of frustration and defeat, thankful no one could see his eyes behind the glasses. Yager's twisted mouth looked like it spit out a curse. Jalen wasn't close enough to hear, but he did hear the ump order

Yager to step up to the plate. Yager's lips tightened. He stepped up. Quintana threw a nasty cutter that he swung at and missed. Yager vacated the box again, and this time his eyes seemed to be pleading.

Jalen swallowed hard, trying to force his brain to cough up the answer.

None came.

Jalen mouthed the words, *I'm sorry*.

Yager's head dropped. He nodded to the ump and stepped back into the box again. Quintana threw a high fastball. Yager let it go for a 1–2 count and stayed in the box. Quintana threw a curve that went too far inside. It was a 2–2 count when Jalen jumped up out of his seat.

"James!" he screamed at the top of his lungs and waved his hands.

Jalen didn't care that people looked at him, as long as Yager did, and he did.

Jalen held up four fingers.

It was going to be a fastball.

He knew it.

70

YAGER NICKED IT FOUL BUT STAYED ALIVE.

Jalen signaled thumbs-down. A sinker was on the way. Yager gave a slight nod and stepped up.

In came the pitch.

Yager tagged it and the ball flew high and long, but not long enough to reach the wall. It was a footrace between the ball and Adam Eaton, the center fielder. Eaton stretched for it, burning up the grass, and barely missed.

Yager made it to second.

The crowd cheered.

Relief flushed through Jalen from head to toe.

From that point on, he felt confident. The night belonged to him, the Yankees, and JY.

Yager went to the plate twice more, hitting a single, then walking. The Yankees won by a score of 2–1. The crowd was bubbling. Yager offered nothing more than a wink to Jalen, when Foxx appeared at the end of their row of seats.

"Well, well! It's the James Yager fan club, bringing more good luck! Well done." Foxx smiled brightly, as if he, too, was a fan of Yager's.

Jalen knew differently, but he couldn't think of a thing to say when the GM invited the four of them to join him in the clubhouse to congratulate the team.

"You mean the locker room?" Cat's mom's face reddened.

Foxx laughed. "No, but right outside in the players' lounge. After they get cleaned up, most of them will have something to eat and let the traffic die down before they head home. We can join them there."

A reporter suddenly appeared at the edge of the wall with a cameraman, Jalen saw two others headed in his direction as well. One was the blond woman from last night.

"Hey, kid. Calamari Kid!" This reporter was a handsome gray-haired man in a Windbreaker. "Did JY eat your dad's food again?"

Before Jalen could speak, the GM stepped up and put a hand in front of the camera. "Sorry, Torin. Jalen is a guest of the Brenneck family. He's not doing interviews."

"Jeffrey, come on," the man pleaded, "it's all over social media, and he talked to FOX last night. I've been waiting all game, and Yager batted a thousand *again*."

"Sorry, Torin." The GM ushered Jalen and his group toward the stairs, holding back the camera with his other hand and turning his back on them once Jalen was out of range.

They clustered at the bottom of the steps to let things clear out. Jalen saw that some of the other people in the VIP section were stealing glances at him, and he wondered if they'd been doing so throughout the game and he simply hadn't noticed because of his focus. He wondered if anyone had seen him giving Yager signals, and it made his mouth dry.

"Okay," Foxx said. "Time to move."

"You better believe I'm good going into the players' lounge," Chris declared. "I'm gonna *be* a player in a couple years anyway."

Foxx chuckled. "Oh, you are, huh?"

"I'm the best player Westchester Little League has ever seen." Chris walked up two steps in front of them and turned around, folding his arms across his barrel chest to make his point. "I broke all Matt Mancini's pitching records, and *he* played four years with Seattle."

Jalen took off his sunglasses and gave Cat a poke in

the back. When she turned, he flashed an angry look and nodded toward Chris to signal to her what a jerk he was. All Cat did was quickly flick her tongue out at him and turn her eyes away.

They reached the main aisle and went down the steps leading to the VIP Club. When they reached the bottom, the GM stopped and looked back and forth between Chris and Jalen. "You two buddies are teammates, huh?"

"The Calamari Kid?" Chris snorted out what might have been a laugh. "I wouldn't say buddies. But we play on the same team. I'm only twelve, and I already throw a seventy-one-mile-an-hour fastball."

Foxx raised an eyebrow. He gave Chris an easy smile and put a hand on his shoulder as he led them all to the left instead of to the right where the VIP Club was. "Oh. Well, yes, that's fast. Come on. We can talk about that. Maybe I can show you the bullpen."

71

JALEN SAT AT A TABLE IN THE PLAYERS' LOUNGE,

fuming.

The GM had simply dumped them there before taking Chris away for a private tour. He didn't even *ask* Jalen or Cat. He just had them sit down while the catering people set up a buffet and said he'd be back in a little while and that they'd have to wait for the players to shower anyway.

Cat and her mom both had their phones out and were typing and scrolling away. He felt it was incredibly rude, but he knew people with phones often tuned out everything around them, so he wasn't surprised when neither of them looked up at the sound of his long, heavy sighs. The lounge soon filled with the smells of roasted meats and red sauce. Tyler Hutt appeared, obviously surprised to see the three of them, even though he offered a winning smile before loading up a tray and sitting down a couple of tables away.

Foxx returned with Chris, who stood tall as he looked down at them. "Well, I got to see my future workplace."

"Let's get some food, shall we?" The GM put a brotherly hand on Chris's shoulder as he addressed them all.

"Oh, I had a sandwich during the game," Cat's mom said. "But you kids can probably eat."

"I'm good." Jalen folded his arms across his chest. He felt like he was in enemy territory, and all he wanted was for Yager to appear and get them away from the devilish GM.

"I'll take a drink." Cat got up and followed Chris and the GM.

Chris loaded his plate with rare beef, golden french fries, and tortellini in red sauce. He had a big Pepsi to wash it all down. He sat across from Jalen without looking at him and attacked his food. Foxx had a plate with some celery and carrot sticks and a dollop of ranch dressing. Cat sat next to Chris, sipping iced tea.

The GM sat next to Jalen, across from Chris and Cat. "That's it, Chris, eat. Enjoy. A boy like you needs to keep his strength up if he's on his way to the Yankees."

Chris looked up and grinned at the GM. Some red sauce leaked from between his teeth before he spoke to Jalen. "I even got to throw a couple pitches in the bullpen."

"You don't throw like any twelve-year-old I've seen," said Jeffrey Foxx.

Chris beamed at him.

"Pretty nice setup, huh?" The GM waved a carrot stick around the lounge, addressing all of them now. "You like being in here? It's pretty special. No one's really allowed back here but the players."

"I was here the other day." Jalen regretted blurting that out the moment it left his lips. He wanted to have something over Chris but instead ended up sounding like just as big a jerk.

The GM's lips curled into a smile, though. "Yes, you were. I haven't forgotten about that."

As the lounge filled up with players, Jalen looked around, thinking how Daniel would have gone wild if he'd been there. While each player gave their little group a strange look, they quickly ignored them or gave the GM a feeble wave before looking away, and the lounge filled with the happy sounds of a victory celebration. Finally Yager appeared, saw them, stopped his laughing, and froze.

Yager wore a look of shock. He approached their table

and stood stiffly facing Jalen and the GM, his hair still wet and glossy from the showers. "Well, this is a surprise."

Foxx's eyes glittered like his teeth. "Well, I figured your little entourage is practically part of the Yankees family, right? I mean, Jalen here seems to be the key to our success. Yours especially, right, James?"

Yager didn't smile back. "I told you he was lucky, Jeffrey. I go four-for-four tomorrow, and you'll be signing me to a new contract, not because you said you would, but because you'd look like a fool dumping me with those kinds of numbers. How'd that be for luck?"

Chris sat chewing with his mouth open like he was watching a good movie. Cat, her mom, and Jalen all squirmed uncomfortably.

"Well, I'm not a betting man," the GM finally said, "but if I were, I wouldn't bet on you batting a thousand tomorrow night."

Foxx wiped his mouth on a linen napkin and stood up.

"Why?" Yager asked. "Because the *odds* are against it?"

The GM laughed and crumpled the napkin before setting it down on the table. "No, not because the odds are against it, James . . . because *I* am."

And he walked away.

72

EACH OF THEM EXCEPT CHRIS WATCHED THE GM
disappear from the lounge.

"Are you going to eat?" Cat's mom asked in a quiet voice.

Yager sighed. "I'm not hungry."

"This stuff is awesome." A little glob of fat flew from Chris's mouth as he spoke, landing on his chin. He dabbed it with a fingertip. It stuck, and he scraped it on his lower lip so it could go the way of everything else on his plate.

Jalen looked at the two adults. "Can we go?"

Cat's mom flicked her eyes at Chris before returning to Yager. "Maybe you could take Jalen?"

"Sure," Yager said. "I'll drop him, then maybe I can join you at Tipton for a drink? Ready, Jalen?"

Jalen was already out of his seat. He glanced at Cat, who seemed to be fascinated by the way Chris ate.

"You two deserve each other," Jalen muttered under his breath as he walked past.

Yager led Jalen straight to the door, but that didn't keep players from giving Yager high fives. Joe Ros held up his phone. "Dude, I saw what you just tweeted. I gotta get some of this calamari. This is the kid, right?"

Yager nodded. "This is Jalen."

Jalen realized it wasn't just Joe Ros who was interested. It seemed half the team was awaiting his response.

"Well, we had a fire, but the diner might be open by Saturday, and anyone can come," Jalen said.

"Worth a try, right?" Hutt leaned over the table and fist-bumped Yager. "I mean, remember when I went on that run back in '09 with the Mets? Ate nothing but chicken, and *that* worked."

"Well, this calamari's working for me, buddy. Hop on board." Yager kept walking, and in a moment they were in the garage with the Lamborghini's doors humming open.

The traffic had thinned out, so it wasn't long before they were back on the highway and racing toward Rockton. Yager had a playlist of old Eagles songs, and he sang along under his breath. Jalen sat silent, waiting for the player to open up about everything that was going on.

After a song called "New Kid in Town," Jalen cleared his throat. "Can I talk to you?"

Yager turned off the music.

"Are you mad at me?" Jalen asked.

Yager flashed him a puzzled look. "Why would I be mad? We're two-thirds of the way to my new contract because of you."

Jalen breathed a sigh of relief. "Well, because Cat and I made you talk to Coach Gamble."

"Oh, that. Yeah, he's a piece of work. Cat was right, though, there's not much he wouldn't do for his kid. What a brute."

"Cat's sure mad, still," Jalen said.

"Well, no one was happy when you made the whole permission-to-miss-practice thing a condition. I wasn't at first either." Yager glanced at him again. "But I get it. I would have been the same way."

"Cat doesn't get it," Jalen said.

"Oh, I bet she does. She's a great kid."

"Well, she's still mad at me."

Yager shrugged. "Must be because of something else."

Jalen winced and knew immediately what that was: his comment about her mom and Yager getting married. "If you see her tonight, can you tell her I'm sorry?"

"For what?" Yager asked.

Jalen couldn't get it out. "Just . . . for everything."

"I can if I see her, Jalen, but if you want my advice, you'll tell her sorry yourself. With women, that's the only way, in my experience," Yager said before pausing. "Listen to me talking like I know what I'm saying. I'm thirty-five years old and still looking."

They were both silent for a minute, the Lamborghini whisking past random cars, avoiding their red taillights like in a video game.

"I mean, what can he do?" Yager spoke like they had been in the middle of an entirely different conversation.

"You mean Foxx?" Jalen asked, even though he thought he knew.

"Yes. Him."

"I don't know," Jalen said. "Ban me from the stadium?"

Yager shook his head.

Jalen bit his lip. "Take away the tickets?"

"Exactly," Yager said.

"But . . . can't you stop him?"

73

"I ALREADY DID." YAGER REACHED INTO THE inside pocket of his coat and produced four blue-and-white tickets. "So now he can't mess us up at the will call window or anything."

"So, we're set," Jalen said.

"Right, it seems like that, but that's what's got me worried." Yager scratched the stubble on his jaw.

"Why?"

"He's not as smart as you, but he's smart, really smart," Yager said. "And I just didn't like the way he acted, bringing you guys into the clubhouse, walking away with a smile like that."

"If he wanted to," Jalen asked, "couldn't he just not sign you? Even if you bat a thousand?"

Yager shook his head. "He wouldn't do that, because I told Tom Verducci what's going on, and he already ran a story on SI.com. Foxx went on record with Verducci about how everything is all about numbers. He's too proud to back down. I don't know, though, he seems so confident that this won't work. It's like he knows something that we don't."

"But what?" Jalen asked.

Yager looked over at him as he steered the car off the highway and into Rockton. "I was hoping you could tell me."

74

JALEN RACKED HIS BRAIN BUT CAME UP WITH nothing.

They wheeled through town and came to the train station. A white halo of light glowed in the night. Dozens of construction lights fixed to posts and machinery illuminated the diner. Men in yellow hard hats flitted in and out. It was as busy as a beehive.

"Wow." Jalen realized he'd been saying that a lot lately. "Thank you for this."

Yager chuckled. "Good old Harvey."

"Harvey?" Jalen wrinkled his nose.

"Harvey Greenland. Big Yankees fan and a friend. It's his construction company." Yager craned his neck as he eased the sports car across the tracks and through the clutter of trucks, generators, and machinery. "He said he could have things back up and running in two days, but he didn't mention two nights. Guy's a beaut."

"You don't have to drive me all the way." Jalen knew the curvy gravel road to his house would leave the Lamborghini coated in dust. "I can walk from here."

"It's not a problem." Gravel clattered against the car's undercarriage until Yager stopped next to Jalen's father's van.

"So," Jalen said. "I forgot to ask, but did you have to give away Daniel's seat for tomorrow, too?"

Yager twisted his lips. "Yes, I did. Man, I know that Chris is just a kid, but what a jerk."

"You should see his dad."

"If he's half as bad as he sounds on the phone, I don't have to see him."

"He is," Jalen said.

"Sounds like a good coach, though." Yager snorted. "From what *he* says, anyway."

"He does win."

"With a pitcher like his kid, it isn't a wonder."

"Were you that good at twelve?" Jalen asked. "Is every major league player?"

Yager peered at him in the light of the dashboard. "You worried about making it to the big leagues?"

Jalen shrugged. "I guess."

"School first, then baseball," Yager said.

"I know," said Jalen.

Yager gave Jalen's shoulder a squeeze. "Jalen, with what you know, and from the swing I saw, you really could make it. It takes a ton of work, though."

"And being on a good team so people notice you." Jalen sighed.

"That's probably true," Yager said. "Well, you better get in. Your dad is probably wondering what happened to you."

Jalen hesitated. "Thanks, Mr. Yager."

"Hey, call me JY, will you?" Yager stifled a yawn. "And I'm the one thanking you, remember? We do this again tomorrow, and everything changes."

"What happens after that?" Jalen asked.

Yager shook his head. "Don't even think about that. Let's just get through tomorrow."

"You say it like there's something wrong," Jalen said.

"I can't say what it is," Yager said. "Just a feeling, and not a feeling I like."

75

JALEN'S DAD SAT WAITING FOR HIM ON THE
couch, reading a paperback spy novel written in Italian.
He smiled at the sight of his son. "Jalen! They won again,
the Yankees. Mr. Yager, he's happy?"

"Yes, Dad."

His father stood up. "Good. Good. The diner, they're
working like . . . beavers. Busy beavers, right?"

Jalen smiled and yawned, and his dad insisted they
both get to bed. Jalen collapsed and didn't wake up until
the six a.m. train shook the pictures on the walls.

School was a circus. By now everyone had heard about
the Calamari Kid—a name Jalen hated, because the truth
was that he was a baseball genius. He wanted to grab

the microphone in the office and shout a schoolwide announcement that luck had nothing to do with it, but he had enough problems with Cat already and didn't need to spoil things with Yager on top of it all.

At lunch Cat sat with Chris and his gang. Daniel gushed about how well Rockets practice had gone without Chris there, and then he peppered Jalen for details about the Yankees game and Yager batting a thousand.

"I told you already, Daniel. It was a 2–2 count, and I knew it was gonna be a sinker." Jalen had told him twice already, once in homeroom, but Daniel was bouncing in his seat.

"Yeah, but what did Yager *do*? What did he look like? I can't believe I *missed* it." Daniel struck his forehead and accidentally knocked over his milk. "Talk about unfair. And Cat doesn't even feel sorry for me. It's like she's blaming me for your rotten behavior."

"Rotten?" Jalen choked on a pretzel. "What did I do that was so bad?"

Daniel tilted his head. "What did you do?"

Jalen glanced over at Cat, pretty as ever and having a laugh with Dirk and Chris. He couldn't control himself. It was too much.

"Where you going?" Daniel's mouth fell open.

Jalen didn't reply. He marched over and took Cat by

the arm. He tugged her up out of her seat and had her halfway to his table before she dug her heels in and cuffed him in the back of the head.

"Ow!" Jalen spun on her.

"What do you think you're doing?" Cat screeched.

Chris was up out of his seat now, and he glowered at Jalen. "Hands off, Calamari."

76

"I GOT THIS, CHRIS." CAT SPOKE THROUGH HER
teeth.

Chris balled his meaty hands into fists. "But—"

"Chris!" Cat directed Chris back to his table with a rigid finger, and he went.

Jalen felt suddenly weak. He leaned toward her to whisper, "You can't do this, Cat. You gotta come back. I'm sorry. Didn't James tell you last night?"

"You mean my future stepfather?" Cat looked around, speaking low, but with all the bitterness of shouting. "When he came over to see my mom?"

"I didn't mean it about them," Jalen said. "It was stupid."

"Yes, it was stupid, but you did mean it." Cat tore her arm loose. "Now leave me alone."

"Cat, you don't have to hang out with me and Daniel, but don't sit with Chris and those goons. You're better than that." Jalen felt sick.

"Why? Because he's big? Because he's not cute like you? It's not about the outside, Jalen. If you don't know that about me by now, you probably never will." Cat stared hard at him with her blue eyes boiling.

Jalen was struck by the fact that she had just called him cute. He wanted to tell her about the name Chris had called him, beneath his rotten breath. He knew Cat would never go for that, but the only thing that came out of his mouth was a gurgle.

"Yeah, see? Nothing to say." Cat scowled and turned to go. "See you later, Jalen. We'll pick you up at the same time. Don't worry. I won't ruin my future stepfather's comeback."

Jalen felt his face burning. Everyone stared. A flash went off as someone took a picture. He could imagine the tagline: *Calamari Kid Crumbles*. He didn't care. He sat back down next to Daniel.

"What was *that*?"

Jalen stared at the table. "Something bad."

"I'll say."

Jalen dragged himself through the rest of the day. At some point—he wasn't sure when—he began to resent Cat. Why did she have to ruin this? He already shared

Yager's ominous feeling that something was going to go wrong. Why couldn't Cat be her good old self? Forgiving and forgetting and *helping?*

When he got off the bus at the end of the day, Jalen grumbled a good-bye to Daniel. There were fewer trucks outside the diner. The crane was gone, and Jalen noticed the glass in the front had been replaced. He went up the front steps before a workman stopped him.

"It's my dad's place," Jalen said.

"Oh yeah." The worker took a closer look at Jalen. "You're that kid. The Calamari Kid."

"Great," Jalen said.

"Hey, just put a hard hat on, okay?" The man handed him a yellow hat. "Boss will have my hide if you don't. Your dad's in the kitchen with him, last I saw."

Jalen wandered in, amazed at how good everything looked. When he entered the kitchen, he had no doubts the diner would be ready for the next night.

Now all they needed was something to celebrate.

77

JALEN LEFT HIS DAD AND WENT BACK HOME TO
change his clothes. He reheated the baked ziti on the
stove and tried to eat some but only managed a few bites
before giving in to his nerves. They had some math homework for the weekend, and he fiddled with that a bit until
it was time to go.

The day had turned cool, so Jalen slipped on his
Yankees hooded sweatshirt and headed down the path.
Cat's mom's Range Rover was already waiting for him
on the corner, and when he saw it he broke into a run,
gravel crunching beneath his sneakers. When he reached
the SUV, he braced himself for a dose of Chris, then flung
open the back door.

Daniel grinned out at him.

"What?" Jalen had no words beyond that.

"Yeah, it's me. Now you got *all* the luck on your side." Daniel pounded his chest.

Jalen looked at Cat, but she still wasn't talking to him. Cat's mom had her hair pulled back into a ponytail, and it was easy to see why Cat was so pretty. The daughter of a woman so beautiful couldn't help it.

"How?" Jalen asked.

"I don't know, but who cares?" Daniel laughed. "Chris called me up and said he wanted me to have his ticket."

"For what? What did you have to give him?"

"*Nothing.* He just did it!"

Jalen felt his stomach sink. "Chris doesn't do anything for nothing."

"He did say he wanted to save up any favors so he could come when the Yankees play the Red Sox." Daniel was obviously trying to help explain the situation.

"I just don't like it," Jalen said. "Cat?"

Jalen was too upset to care about their feud.

"Tell Jalen that maybe he was wrong about Chris after all." Cat turned and spoke just to Daniel. "Tell him he shouldn't judge a book by its cover. Most of all, remind him he's got a job to do, and we all hope he'll focus on that."

Cat turned back around facing front.

Jalen wanted to pinch her. He was so mad, he pinched himself.

Daniel saw him and said, "Dude, that's not right."

They parked in the same VIP spot in the garage next to the stadium and went directly to the stadium like old pros. They had some time and felt comfortable enough to sit in the VIP Club at a table so Daniel, Cat, and her mom could eat some of the fine food. Jalen simply got a ginger ale that he sipped. None of them asked him to explain. They knew the pressure he was under and it made their whole group quiet, even Daniel.

Jalen did see the old-timer he'd spoken to on Wednesday night, but he was busy at his carving station and took no notice of Jalen. There was no sign of the GM, even when they went out into the stands and took their seats next to the dugout. Jalen cast a long look up at the owner's box, and no one was looking down with any binoculars that he could see, but he took out his sunglasses anyway.

Yager seemed nervous as well. When the Yankees took infield warm-ups, he fumbled two grounders and threw wide of first base another time. Jalen tried to read Yager's face, hoping to see a positive outlook that Jalen didn't feel himself. It was weird. Everything should have been smooth. Daniel had replaced Chris and now sat next to

Jalen, patting his back and telling him he was "the Man." There was still no sign of Foxx and his nasty scowl. All should be well, but it was too easy.

Everyone stood for the national anthem, and when Jalen took his seat, he pushed all the doubts and questions from his mind. Cat was right about what she'd said in the car; he had a job to do, a job that could change the lives of not just James Yager and Jalen DeLuca, but his dad too, and that was what enabled him to dial in and concentrate.

Michael Pineda took the hill for the Yankees and sat the first three White Sox batters down. The crowd roared its approval. The Sox sent Dylan Fanale to the mound. Fanale had rocketed up through the minors the previous season, and he had looked like the real deal so far. Jalen knew he had a big arm, but without the movement Holton or even Quintana could put on the ball. Jalen knew Fanale killed people with his changeup. But if Yager knew when the changeup was coming, he could slaughter it.

The Sox finished their warm-up at the bottom of the first, and Ellsbury stepped up to the plate. Jalen narrowed his eyes and leaned forward to study Fanale. On a 3–2 count, Ellsbury fouled down the right field line. The pitch most likely should have been the four-seam fastball, but Jalen suddenly knew Fanale was going to throw his curveball.

He did, and Ellsbury missed it, swinging for the wall.

The next two Yankee batters went down as well, Gardner on a pop fly and Hall whiffing on three in a row. If this kept up, Yager might only need to go three-for-three a second night in a row. Perfection would be that much easier.

The first thing that went wrong happened with the third Sox batter in the top of the second. Pineda had put the first two down when the third batter dribbled a grounder to Yager at second. Yager snapped it up and cranked his hips as he fired the ball harder than he had to. Tollerson leaped and stretched, but nothing could have let him snag such an errant throw.

The crowd murmured, then rallied and cheered Pineda on.

The magic had been broken, though. The Sox scored two runs, and it was Yager who'd given them life. It made what he did at the plate that much more important, and Jalen knew Yager would be feeling it. Anyone would.

The good news was, Jalen had Fanale all figured out, and Yager just might get the chance to redeem himself in the bottom of the second.

Fanale walked Tegan Tollerson right out of the gate,

making a Yager at bat highly likely. Jalen clenched his teeth and watched, muttering the pitches to himself. Daniel kept giving him hopeful looks, and even Cat looked over with a question in her eyes. Jalen didn't smile at her, but he gave a businesslike thumbs-up.

Then it was time.

Yager gave Jalen a quick glance from the on-deck circle, and Jalen answered with a forced smile. James smiled too and circled the plate before staring hard at Jalen.

That was when two thick-necked stadium security guards appeared to take Jalen away.

78

THE GUARDS' FACES MIGHT HAVE BEEN CUT FROM
blocks of ice.

"Excuse me, Jalen DeLuca?" The taller of the two spoke. "You need to come with us."

Jalen obeyed at the sight of them. He jerked up out of his seat like a puppet on strings.

"Wait one minute." Cat's mom rose from her seat as well, blocking Jalen. "What's this all about?"

The action on the field didn't stop. Jalen heard Fanale's pitch pop into the catcher's mitt.

"Strike!" called the umpire.

Jalen took a quick glance at Yager, who had stepped out of the box and was staring at him. Yager's face had lost all its color.

"This young man stole some stadium property, and the GM needs to talk with him about it," the shorter guard said.

"What are you even talking about?" Cat's mom raised her voice. "We were given these tickets by James Yager!"

"Mr. Foxx told us if there were any questions, we were to show you this." The guard reached into the pocket of his dark-blue Windbreaker and removed a tiny bottle filled about a third of the way with dirt.

Jalen recognized in his own block-letter handwriting YANKEE STADIUM INFIELD, as well as Yager's signature.

"It's dirt," Cat's mom said to the guards.

The shorter guard pointed at Jalen. "Yeah, and he was specifically told to put it back."

"Is this true?" Cat's mom asked.

Jalen nodded, and she let the guard by. The guards took him by each arm. Jalen thought he might throw up.

"Wait," Cat's mom said, "I'm coming with you. Cat and Daniel, you wait right here. I'll be back."

Jalen couldn't help turning, glaring at Daniel, and spitting his words. "You said you didn't have to give Chris anything to get him to give you his ticket."

Daniel's face flushed. He shrugged innocently and held up his hands. He looked confused and upset, but he didn't deny it.

Another pitch smacked into the catcher's glove out on the field behind Jalen.

"Strike!" barked the ump, signaling strike two.

Jalen couldn't even look at the action on the field, and he choked on his words before turning away.

"Daniel, you ruined everything."

79

THE GUARDS GENTLY TUGGED JALEN'S ARMS, AND
he moved between them up the stairs with Cat's mom following closely, muttering to herself that the whole thing was unbelievable.

When they got to the top of the steps, the sound of Yager's bat nicking the ball foul got even the guards' attention, allowing Jalen to look past Cat's mom and back down at his friends.

Cat and Daniel were both staring at him, as were most of the fans sitting in the premium seats. They seemed to care as much about the Calamari Kid being taken away by the authorities as Yager's performance at the plate. Jalen ignored the stares, because his eyes were locked on Daniel.

His best friend still wore a look of complete stupor. But now, one of Daniel's hands was open, palm up, helpless, and facing the sky. In the other hand, held high for Jalen to see, was Daniel's bottle of lucky stadium dirt that he had removed from his pocket. Daniel then made a grand pointing gesture with his empty hand to make sure Jalen saw that indeed, Daniel *hadn't* given away his dirt.

Jalen gasped when he realized what had happened.

It all came together like the numbers on the billboard in his brain. Cat getting so friendly with Chris. Cat saying he reminded her of her brother, Austin. Cat upset about her mom and Yager maybe becoming an item. Cat furious with Jalen for various reasons, including the scene in the cafeteria.

Cat was playing for the other team.

80

"LET'S GO, KID." THE TALL GUARD TUGGED AT HIM,
and Jalen had to go.

They passed an usher and then slogged down more concrete steps, heading for the VIP Club and most likely the elevators beyond.

Inside the club Jalen saw his friend Mr. Moses, who'd carved him a prime rib sandwich two nights ago. The older man pressed his lips tight and shook his head sadly at the sight of Jalen. Jalen wagged his head to say that it wasn't true, he wasn't a bad kid. The motion died quickly, though, because deep down Jalen knew he really had taken the dirt, and he really had hid it from Yager, letting him believe that he'd put it all back until Daniel exposed him by asking JY to sign the bottles. So he had to ask himself: Could a thief and a liar really be a good kid?

He hung his head as an answer to his own question.

Out they went, into the concrete tunnel, and waited for the elevator in silence.

"Don't worry, Jalen," Cat's mom suddenly said. "We'll get this all straightened out."

The elevator dinged and the doors rumbled open. Jalen couldn't reply.

They stepped in and turned around. There was an operator in the elevator; otherwise they were alone. The doors had just begun to close when Daniel appeared out of nowhere.

He darted into the elevator car, jamming a finger down his throat in the same instant.

With a gag and a heave, Daniel lost his slushies all over the two security guards. The slick sound of stomach juice and the smell of acid and hot dog chunks shocked everyone.

With his free hand, Daniel pushed Jalen out through the closing doors.

One of the guards made a move for Jalen, but his feet slipped on the mess and flew right out from under him. As the doors thumped shut, Jalen heard the guard hit the floor with a howl.

Jalen stood motionless for a moment, just as the elevator operator must have been frozen inside the car. He looked around.

The tunnel was empty and he was alone.

Jalen took off like a rocket.

81

JALEN'S INSTINCTS CARRIED HIM BACK THE WAY
he came.

He was already six steps into the VIP Club when he realized there was nothing to go back to at the seats. Cat was there, but she was now the enemy, and it wouldn't be long before more guards came to take him away.

He froze and turned, wondering if he could find his way through the maze to the players' parking garage. Maybe he could hide in Yager's car?

The thought vanished instantly, like the bad idea that it was, and Jalen found himself staring into the face of Mr. Moses, the old man in the tall white hat.

"You look to be in some trouble." Mr. Moses looked around quickly, speaking quietly in his low voice.

There were shouts coming from the hallway now. The guards were back off the elevator.

"Here. Get in." Mr. Moses stepped around his station and raised the table's skirt, exposing the cart's legs on wheels and a shelf below big enough for Jalen to sit on with crossed legs.

Mr. Moses fixed the skirt back around the trolley, enveloping Jalen in a gloomy light. Jalen heard footsteps clapping the floor. The toes of two beetle-black shoes appeared at the edge of the skirt, messy from Daniel's vomit. Jalen heard heavy breathing, and the odor of throw-up crept beneath the skirt so that Jalen had to clench his throat with both hands to keep from gagging.

"Hey," one of the guards said, "did you see the kid?"

Jalen froze.

"Kid?" Mr. Moses rumbled softly. "What kid?"

"He must have gone back out into the stands," the other guard said. "Come on!"

"Maybe he stayed in the tunnel. This guy would've seen him."

"Mr. Foxx is gonna have our hides."

"No one's gonna blame us. The kid barfed all over us, Jim. And the mom's making excuses for him."

"I think that woman—the mom—stepped in front of me on purpose, you believe that?"

"Come on."

They clomped off, back the way they came.

After a long minute, Jalen heard Mr. Moses whisper, "They're gone. I'm gonna wheel you outta here, so hang on."

Slowly the cart began to move. Jalen held on to the legs to keep himself still. They'd gone quite a ways—Jalen figured they had to be nearly out of the club—when a voice called out behind them.

"Hey! Stop!"

It was a high-pitched voice, not of a guard, but something just as bad.

It was Cat.

"Hello, miss," Mr. Moses rumbled. "Miss? Hey, miss . . ."

The skirt hiding Jalen was torn aside.

There stood Cat, eyes blazing.

"I *found* you."

82

JALEN FROZE, NOT FROM TERROR, BUT FROM
disappointment. Part of him didn't care that the game
was up. If Cat was against him, everything else seemed to
matter a lot less.

She reached for Jalen's arm, and he let her tug him out
from under the roast station. "Come on, this way. Fast!"

Her voice had the tone of a fellow prisoner on the run,
so Jalen had hope.

"Thanks, mister," Cat said to Mr. Moses. "I got him now."

She had him, all right. Cat hurried Jalen toward the
stadium, talking as they went. "We can get you lost in the
crowd. I'll stash you, and then you can call me. I'll signal
James."

They burst outside. An usher said, "Hey!"

Cat didn't slow down, and Jalen was moving fast now too, keeping up. They went up and up, into the concession area and a sea of people. They found some stairs and kept climbing. When they reached the third tier, Cat led him out into the stands again. An usher stood watching the game, but Cat marched past him like they belonged. Now they went down, then over—excusing themselves as they bumped past people's knees—into a spot where six seats sat empty. Out on the field, Yager stood atop third with Gregorius on first and Ellsbury at the plate.

Ellsbury's bat cracked, and down below, the miniature shapes of men moved around the diamond, pushing Yager across home plate, exciting the crowd.

Hope sprang up in Jalen's heart. "He made it on."

Cat nodded. "Pulled a shot right down the third base line. Are you going to be able to read the pitches from up here?"

Jalen squinted down at the tiny figures. "It's better when I can see their faces, but I should be able to get most of them anyway."

"Because I think this is about as close as you can safely get." Cat looked around, then leaned forward, peering down at the seats they'd been in. "I better get back and find my mom. She's probably having a fit."

"And Daniel," Jalen said. "I wonder what happened to him. I can't believe he actually sprang me free. Only Daniel could come up with an idea as crazy as puking on everyone."

"Well . . ." Cat looked at her hands.

"It was your idea?"

She looked at him with those fiery blue eyes and smirked. "We had to do something."

"Cat, I thought you were mad at me," Jalen said.

"I *am* mad at you, Jalen." She looked back at her hands. "I was, anyway."

"I'm really sorry, Cat. I didn't mean it. I was stupid."

She smiled. "It's okay. Friends forever, right? That's why I'm here."

Cat held out her hand. Jalen shook it and pulled her into a hug. "Best friends forever."

Jalen let her go. "But how did they get that bottle of dirt?"

"Must have been from Chris," Cat said. "He wanted Daniel's and offered to trade Daniel for his game ticket. Daniel wouldn't give his up, but I wanted Daniel to be with us, so I gave mine to Chris."

"But how did Foxx get it?" Jalen asked.

Cat shrugged. "The two of them were pretty chummy the other day. Maybe Foxx had Chris on the lookout for it, or maybe Chris just saw an opportunity to suck up to the Yankees GM and gave him a call. Getting it would be easy. Just send someone up the road to pick it up and bring it back."

Jalen gritted his teeth. "That rat."

Cat handed him her phone. "Let's not worry about all that now. Let's just get in place so when James is up again, I can get him that signal. I've got my mom's phone cued up. All you have to do is dial it."

Jalen insisted they review the signals before he let her go. Gardner's slow grounder was kept in the infield, just barely. Frazier held the ball, and the bases were loaded with Yankees. The crowd got to its feet, and that let Cat slip past. Jalen watched her disappear up the steps without looking back.

Hall popped out, ending the inning with the Yankees down 2–1. Jalen didn't pay much attention to the Yankees in the field. He kept scanning the VIP section for a sign of Cat and her mom, still also wondering about Daniel. His throat grew tight from time to time at the thought of them all being detained, but it didn't seem possible that the security guards would dare to do that to Cat's mom. He doubted they'd think of him using Cat as his substitute for signals.

It was a brilliant plan.

Still, the game continued with no sign of Cat.

The Yankees gave up another run before ending the top of the third and jogging to the dugout. Jalen strained his eyes, but the four seats they'd occupied next to the on-deck circle remained empty. He tried to pay attention to Fanale's pitching, but it was hard to concentrate with those empty seats staring up at him. Tollerson went down swinging, and Hutt drove one deep into center field, but not deep enough. Joe Ros got up with two outs, and Yager appeared in the circle.

Still the seats sat empty.

Joe Ros battled to a full count. Jalen began to sweat. Yager had gotten his first hit, but what were the odds of him getting a second without Jalen's help?

It felt odd to be relieved when Joe Ros struck out on a shaky call. The fans began to boo the ump. Joe Ros jawed at the ump too as he stomped back to the dugout. Jalen seemed to be the only fan in the whole stadium sitting quietly.

He had half an inning left. That was it. If Cat didn't appear back in their seats, Yager would be on his own.

83

THE YANKEES' DEFENSE HELD, AND THE PLAYERS
returned to the dugout much too soon for Jalen, because
Cat still hadn't shown up. Yager loaded his bat and stood
swinging as Fanale heated up his arm with a few fastballs. Yager took the doughnut off his bat and turned to
the stands. Just in time, Cat raced down the steps and
stood face-to-face with Yager at the wall. Yager paused,
but only for a moment before circling the plate and stepping up to bat.

Jalen fumbled with his phone, dialing Cat's mom.

As he watched, Cat's mom, along with Daniel, appeared
and sat down next to Cat.

Cat answered. "What have you got?"

"I . . . nothing yet." The whole thing had flustered Jalen.

Fanale wound up and threw a low outside strike. Yager only watched it.

"Jalen? Jalen!"

"You don't have to yell," Jalen whispered into the phone. "I'm watching. I'm *trying*."

Yager delayed as much as he could but finally had to step back into the box.

"Jalen?"

Jalen shook his head. "I . . . I want to say fastball, but I don't know. I'm so far away, Fanale looks like an ant."

Fanale threw a fastball that went too wide, giving Yager a 1–1 count. He stepped out and looked at Cat.

"Oh, Jalen, *please*."

"It's . . ."

Yager stepped back into the box.

"Fastball!"

Jalen couldn't see if Cat signaled or not. He couldn't tell if Yager got it, but he swung at the fastball, nicking it foul into the backstop.

Yager stepped out of the box.

"Oh, Jalen," Cat said. "He looks so mad. That was too late."

"Two thumbs-up, Cat."

"Thumbs?"

"Up. Signal two thumbs-up. Changeup. That's the pitch, Cat. Go!"

Even from the third tier Jalen could see Cat signaling that. Yager stepped into the box. In came the pitch.

Yager hit it over the left field wall.

84

THE CROWD ROARED.

Jalen jumped to his feet and pumped his empty fist into the air, overjoyed that strangers around him all wanted to exchange high fives. If they only knew!

"Yes! Yes! Yes!" he shouted into the phone as Cat screamed with delight. Jalen could hear Daniel and Cat's mom cheering as well.

"We did it!" Cat cried.

"We did. We did." Jalen was breathless.

"Hey," Cat said. "How's my battery?"

"Your what?"

"The battery. My phone."

Jalen checked it and swallowed. "Cat, it says fourteen percent."

"Shoot. I thought so," she said. "Okay, no problem. Just shut it down until James gets up again. Just hold the side button and swipe it to power down. When you're ready, hold that same button again and it'll come on. My pass code is 1923, the year of the Yankees' first title."

Jalen looked around, suddenly uncomfortable alone in the big crowd. With Cat on the phone he didn't feel that way, but there was nothing else he could do. "Uh . . . okay. I'll call you back when he's up."

"You'll be fine," Cat said.

"Sure."

Things settled back down, and Fanale went to work on the rest of the Yankees lineup so that the inning ended with nothing more than Yager's run, preserving a 3–2 lead for the White Sox. Pineda countered with a hot inning of his own, giving up nothing more than a single before the Yankees left the field.

Jalen looked around. He might as well have been invisible in the big crowd, and he let out a sigh, then chuckled to himself. Yager might only get up one more time, twice at most unless they went into extra innings. He was that close to a jackpot. He fretted just a bit about the Rockets' tournament in White Plains tomor-row and what time they'd be finished and if he could get to the celebration of the Silver Liner's grand reopening. He wanted to see the look on his father's face, but he supposed he didn't have to be there to turn the attention into a gold mine.

Jalen sat there, breathing easy, counting the money he and his father would collect, when he noticed an usher moving down the aisle to his left. Everyone's attention was on the game, but the usher seemed to be searching the crowd for someone. Instinctively, Jalen looked to his right. There was an usher in that aisle too, also walking slowly down the steps. Jalen looked left. That usher was closer now, but looking the other way.

When he looked right, that usher stared straight at him, squinted, and raised a walkie-talkie to his mouth. The usher stood frozen. His big, dark eyes swelled behind his glasses, and they didn't waver from Jalen. Jalen looked left again. That usher had moved past Jalen, down a couple rows.

The usher to his right gave a shout. "Hey! Marvin! It's him! Marvin!"

Just then Gardner punched a grounder through the 3-4 hole and the crowd erupted, drowning out the usher's cries. Jalen bolted from his seat and went left. He bumped through people's knees, saying, "Sorry" as he went. By the time the crowd noise subsided, Jalen was in the aisle and charging up the steps. He heard more shouting behind him.

"Kid! Stop! Get that kid!"

Jalen's heart galloped in his chest. Adrenaline fueled his legs. He darted into the tunnel. When he hit the concourse, he went right, away from the usher who'd spotted him. He just had to get away. He could figure out where else to go later.

Thoughts of a disguise flashed through his brain.

When he rounded the corner, a man the size of a small hippo with a bucket of popcorn cuddled up under each arm tried to avoid Jalen. Jalen tried to avoid him, too. They ended up shifting the same way. Jalen struck the man and popcorn exploded into the air before snowing down on them both. Jalen's foot hit a melted patch of sno-cone, and down he went.

In an instant he was up, but as he bolted, the big man caught him by the arm.

"Hey! What's wrong with you?"

Jalen rebounded into him, surprised by his strength.

Before he could shake loose, someone grabbed his collar.

Jalen spun and saw the shiny gold badge of one of New York's finest.

85

THIS TIME THERE WAS NO ONE TO MAKE A MESS
and save the day. Daniel and Cat and her mom didn't even
know Jalen was in trouble, and the policeman's grip was
like an iron claw.

"Heard you're a runner." The cop chewed his gum
loudly and spoke in a tone that suggested he was about to
burst out in laughter.

Jalen shrugged.

The usher who'd spotted him arrived and showed the
cop a picture of Jalen that someone had taken from his TV
interview after the first White Sox game, sunglasses and all.

"That's him. I spotted him." The usher swelled with
pride.

"Good stuff," said the cop, and off they went, not to the owner's box where Jalen expected, but down into the guts of the stadium, where Jalen had been with Yager on their first trip and just yesterday with the GM.

They stopped outside Joe Girardi's office, and the cop knocked. Jalen was confused because it seemed odd that the team manager would leave the game to attend to Jalen. When Jalen entered under the firm hand of the policeman, he was surprised to see Foxx, with his feet up on the desk, staring at him hard.

86

THE GM'S EYES SWIRLED WITH A MIXTURE OF bitterness and triumph. "Thought you'd outsmart me?"

He tapped the side of his head and chuckled. "Not likely. You think those glasses covered up what you're doing? The Yankees would be embarrassed if the team got caught stealing signs. If the team is embarrassed, I'll look bad. You're not going to make me look bad. Neither is Yager.

"Besides." Foxx grinned. "I'll prevail eventually. I told you. It's all about smarts. You can sit down. You're not going anywhere."

Jalen took a seat in front of the desk and removed his glasses. Joe Girardi had pictures of his wife and children all around. On the wall was a picture of him with George

Steinbrenner's son Hal and the World Series trophy.

"JY can't hit without you." Foxx said. "His skills are gone. It happens. He'll move on, and you? You're finished too." He swung his legs down from the desk and stood.

"Lucky calamari. Who came up with that?"

The GM crossed the room and reached behind the flat-screen TV resting on a shelf. He fiddled with something, then held up a TV cable for Jalen to see before stuffing it in his pocket.

The GM pulled open the office door and paused. "Calamari gives me diarrhea."

He closed the door behind him with a soft click.

Jalen tried to listen for the sound of his footsteps, but the door was thick.

He waited a few moments, then tried it. The handle turned. Soft and slow, Jalen kept turning it. He couldn't believe his luck, and he laughed to himself at Foxx thinking he was so smart only to forget something so simple and stupid.

Jalen eased the door open a crack. Nothing happened.

He gathered himself to run, then swung open the door.

"Peekaboo." The NYPD officer smiled up at him from a chair in the hall.

Jalen knew his face must have changed color, but he thought quick. "I have to use the bathroom."

"No problem." The officer led him to a bathroom and waited outside.

When they returned to the manager's office, the officer closed the door behind him. Jalen stood looking around. He remembered a James Bond movie and examined the air vent. No way could he fit through. There was no other way out.

Jalen's breathing became short and shallow. Yager could be up at any time.

Then he remembered Cat's phone. Foxx hadn't taken it. Jalen fished it out of his pocket and fumbled with the button to turn it on. It asked for Cat's code: 1923. Jalen entered it and the screen came to life.

He dialed Cat.

She might know what to do.

87

"I DON'T MIND YOU CALLING, BUT YOU GOTTA BE careful with that battery." That was how Cat answered her mother's phone, in a hushed voice.

"He got me," Jalen said.

"Who? What are you talking about?" Cat's whisper rose.

"Foxx. They found me, Cat. Every usher in the stadium was looking. They did a sweep. I tried to run, but I ran into some guy and tripped and a cop got me."

"Where are you?" she asked.

"Foxx put me in Joe Girardi's office."

"So, you're still here," she said. "That's good."

Jalen could feel her thinking. "There's no way you can get me. The cop is right outside the door. I already tried."

Jalen knew she was thinking. He heard the crowd cheer in the background. "What happened?"

"Joe Ros just made a diving catch on a foul ball." Cat spoke in a regular voice. "He nearly fell into the TV camera pit."

"Is the inning over?"

"Yes."

"Is Yager gonna be up?" Jalen asked.

"Yes."

"Cat, what are we gonna do?"

"I'm thinking, Jalen."

"Think faster."

"You're the genius," she snapped.

"Cat, please . . ."

Jalen looked around at all the pictures of famous people, the baseballs and bats on the shelves, the pictures of men with trophies and Joe Girardi's family. Here he was, at the center of it all—the lifeblood of the Yankees—but he might as well have been in a spaceship, cut loose from the world.

He gave his head a short shake, because he wasn't cut loose. He was connected to Cat.

Then she spoke, excited and joyful. "I got it."

Jalen clenched the phone and waited.

88

"IS THERE A TV IN THE OFFICE?" CAT ASKED.

Jalen's heart sank. "There is, but Foxx took the cable."

"He is smart," Cat said, her voice hushed again, "but so are we. Is there a charger there? An iPhone charger?"

"I don't know. What's it look like?" Jalen felt panicked by the question, because iPhones weren't part of the life of a boy whose father ran a bankrupt diner.

"A white cable," she said, "maybe black, with a little thingy on the end like a flat tab no bigger than a pencil eraser. Look for a plug in the wall or on the desk, an electric socket that has maybe a little square thing plugged in it that has that cable. The cable isn't much bigger than a thick piece of spaghetti."

Jalen's throat tightened. He saw nothing of the kind.

"Why do we need it?"

"For the power," Cat said. "We need to FaceTime, but it will use up all the battery."

"FaceTime?" The term rang a bell, but that was all.

"With iPhones you can talk and see the person too," Cat said. "It's like Skype. It's instant video. Trust me, Jalen. This will work. You have to find a charger cable."

"Yeah, well, what if there isn't one?" Jalen kept looking around the room. There were plugs on the wall and even a bank of them under the desk, but no cords like she was describing.

"Nothing," he said, exasperated.

"There has to be," she hissed. "Is there a computer?"

"Yes, on his desk."

"Check that," she said. "Is there a cable plugged into it?"

Jalen saw the thick white spaghetti strand, and his heart leaped. "Yes. It's here."

"Awesome! Plug it into the slot in the bottom edge of the phone."

Jalen fumbled with the cord and plugged it in, proud. "Done."

"Super. Is it charging? Do you see a little lightning bolt? Upper-right corner of the screen, right inside the little battery icon."

"Uhh, no," Jalen said. "I see the battery. It's red and it says fourteen percent."

"Maybe you have to boot the computer. Wait, forget it. Yager's up." Cat sounded suddenly frantic. "Just hang up. I'm going to FaceTime you. Just hit the green button to accept the FaceTime call when it rings. Hang up, Jalen."

Jalen fumbled with the phone. His fingers were unsure, but he hung up and waited in the vast silence of the office.

The phone beeped sharply at him, like an angry electronic insect. Jalen accepted the call. Cat's face appeared. She had earbuds in, as if she were listening to music on the phone. She still spoke low but forcefully. "Okay, good. Now, you watch. I'll point this at Fanale. When you see it, you tell me. I'll signal to James."

The screen flung around, and Jalen saw the White Sox pitcher on the mound.

"Good?" she asked.

"Yes, I see him." Jalen was so flustered, he couldn't think.

"What's the pitch? What's the pitch?" Cat's voice screeched at him.

Fanale wound up.

"I don't know, Cat!" Jalen yelled at her as Fanale delivered a ball. "Stop barking at me. I can't just flip it on like that!"

"Well, you need to." Her voice softened, maybe because it was a 1–0 count. "Please, Jalen. Please. I want this for you."

Jalen swallowed and tried to focus. "Cat, show me the scoreboard. Try to hold it still."

"Okay. I am."

Jalen tried to breathe deep. It was the bottom of the seventh. One out. A runner on first. White Sox still had a 3–2 lead. Fanale had already thrown eighty-eight pitches.

"Okay," Jalen said, "now show me the pitcher."

She adjusted the phone just as Fanale shook off the catcher. He shook him off again before nodding.

"Jalen?"

"Trying," he said.

Fanale wound up and threw.

Jalen heard the pitch smack the catcher's mitt and the ump bark, calling a strike.

"James is looking at me." Cat sounded like she might cry. "And I don't know what to do."

"Just keep the phone still." Jalen heard his voice as if he were outside of himself. He absorbed what he saw. Fanale nodding. Fanale looking off the runner on first.

"Fastball!" Jalen exploded. "Four fingers, Cat!"

The phone jiggled.

A bat cracked.

The crowd cheered.

"Cat! What happened? What happened?"

Jalen shook the phone, joy flooding him.

Cat's face appeared, grinning enormously. "You did it! James—"

The screen went black.

The phone powered down.

A battery figure appeared briefly with a red line before Jalen saw nothing.

He sat alone, breathing loud, as dread surged through his veins like poison.

He had no power, and no way to recharge the phone, but Yager would still have one final at bat.

89

JALEN SCOURED THE OFFICE, TRYING TO BE AS neat as he could. He began to sweat because he realized that out in the stadium the clock was ticking away. Pitches were being thrown, outs made, balls hit, everything bringing the lineup back toward a final Yager at bat. The desk drawers were locked and he thought about trying to force them open, but he knew that—combined with the dirt he'd taken—would sink him as a thief no matter how things turned out. Also, he didn't see anything he could use to force them open anyway.

"Think, Jalen. Think." His words fell dead around him.

He turned the computer on and off, remembering what Cat said and realizing that he needed the password to boot it up and engage the USB power supply.

"Password," he said aloud.

This was Joe Girardi's office and his own computer. There was no need for anything crazy. He'd just do something simple, like Cat's phone code: 1923, when the Yankees won their first title.

Jalen tried that.

Nothing.

He looked around at the pictures, and his eyes fell on a blown-up image of Girardi with the number 28 on his back, celebrating with his team. Twenty-eight was the manager's number, so he tried Joe28, then Baseball28, Girardi28, then Yankees28.

Nothing.

He tried Password, then Password1, then Password28, and Password1234 before banging his head down on the desk. He was so close. It was right here in front of him.

He was only a password away.

He opened his eyes and looked at the wall. The picture of Girardi and Hal Steinbrenner stared back at him, grinning.

"Twenty-seven," Jalen said. "Not twenty-eight, twenty-seven."

Joe Girardi had been number 27 when he won the World Series.

Jalen straightened up and began typing.

It took several attempts, but it was Baseball27 that finally did it.

The machine booted up. The phone buzzed. Jalen picked it up and saw the battery picture with a big white lightning bolt filling its center.

A few moments later, he powered up the phone and dialed Cat.

90

"WHAT HAPPENED?" CAT WAS FRANTIC. "JALEN, where *were* you?"

"I had to get the power on. Forget that now. What's going on?"

"Bottom of the ninth," she said, turning the camera in her mom's phone toward the field. "Gardner struck out. Hall's on first and Tollerson's up. We're still down by a run. They put Robertson in to close the ninth."

Jalen saw the former Yankees pitcher on the hill for the White Sox. He closed his eyes. The numbers were all there. The 34.4 percent strikeout rate jumped out at him, as did Robertson's home and away ERA. He was twice as effective at home, and this was no longer his home. While

David Robertson was known for his wicked curve, Jalen knew it was the cutter he'd recently brushed up on that made him even more dangerous. He'd hit ninety-six miles an hour with his fastball, but typically it came in between ninety-two and ninety-three.

"He uses a curve," Jalen told Cat. "That signal is just to draw a big *C* in the air with your finger."

"Got it," she said.

"If I can read it."

"You will." Cat didn't sound entirely confident.

Jalen watched as Tegan Tollerson fell behind on an 0–2 count and fought to protect the plate, fouling three balls before Robertson sat him with the curve. Jalen felt like he wasn't close to knowing the pitches with Robertson, but there were two outs now, and he couldn't help that giddy feeling that Yager might not have to bat a fourth time. He'd be three-for-three. Perfect. He'd get his contract, and it'd be a happy ending for them all.

Hutt went to the plate and popped one over the third baseman's head for a single on the first pitch. Jalen swallowed hard.

He needed to focus on the pitcher, not how great things would be if Joe Ros didn't get on base. The Yankees catcher could also knock it out of the park, ending the game that way. That was what Jalen began to root for. Joe Ros let two fastballs go wide, neither of which Jalen predicted.

"You getting it?" Cat asked.

"Just keep the picture on Robertson." Jalen propped the phone up against a paperweight on the desk and grabbed his hair with both hands. He had to stop wishing for Joe Ros to hit a home run or be called out and focus on the *pitcher*.

Robertson threw a curve that Joe Ros fouled.

Jalen tugged at his hair, willing his genius to kick in.

"One and two count," he said aloud, closing his eyes to see the billboard of numbers. When he opened them, he wanted to say fastball but was glad he didn't. It was a cutter that Joe Ros let go, a ball inside, making it a 2–2 count.

Jalen studied Robertson as he prepared to throw.

"Curve," he whispered.

It was a curve. Jalen had it.

Joe Ros hit it, dropping it perfectly into the left field hole over the shortstop's leap, loading the bases.

Then the unthinkable happened.

91

IT WASN'T FOXX BARGING IN ON HIM.

It wasn't the phone going dead or Cat being dragged off by security guards as he'd been.

It was Robin Ventura, the White Sox manager, approaching the mound with Carlos Rodon in tow. Rodon was the young first-round pick from a couple of years ago on a steady climb.

"Oh, boy," Cat said into the phone. "What do you know about him?"

"Lefty," Jalen said, trying to dig up the numbers in his brain, knowing he was in trouble if he had to start predicting pitches immediately. He hadn't even gotten Robertson figured out, and now he had to start all over.

"Decent fastball. Been working on his changeup, but his best pitch is a slider. Against James on the right side of the plate, that thing will be filthy, looks just like a fastball, then breaks low and inside at the last instant."

"Can you predict it?" Cat asked.

"I have no idea," Jalen said.

"But sometimes you get it right away, don't you?" Her voice cracked.

"Sometimes." Jalen clenched his teeth and watched Rodon throw three warm-up pitches before Yager stepped to the plate.

"Anything?" Cat asked.

"Just keep it steady, Cat." He was annoyed by even the slight movement of the camera.

"Have fun, Jalen," she said in her hushed voice. "Remember you told me Jeter said, 'Have fun'?"

Rodon threw a strike, fastball on the high side, but down the middle. Yager swung late and missed.

"How could this be fun?" Jalen asked bitterly.

"Because it *is*." Cat was being her usual stubborn self. "It's baseball. It's just a game."

Jalen laughed. He couldn't even express how much more than a game this was. It was silly that she didn't see it. He kept laughing; it had him now in its grip.

"What's so funny?" Cat sounded annoyed.

Rodon threw that dirty slider. Yager swung and missed, making it 0–2, a nearly impossible situation. Perfect for Foxx, though. It would show that Yager's recent run was really just a final burst of light before it ended, a nostalgic glimpse of what he used to be before Foxx pulled the plug to make way for the future: Charlie Cunningham, the strapping young infielder.

"Jalen, he's looking at me," Cat said. "*Please*. Give me something. Anything! You've got to *try*."

"Anything?" Jalen kept laughing, nearly crazy now, because he felt he would cry. Then he saw something, or thought he did. He couldn't be certain, but he said, "Sure. Anything. Fun, right? Give him two thumbs-up."

"Two thumbs . . . a changeup?" Doubt flooded Cat's voice. "Not another slider?"

"Why? Signal a changeup." Jalen chuckled like a madman. Tears welled in his eyes now, because he expected it was all over. He sniffed, but kept laughing. "For fun."

92

CAT SIGNALED TWO THUMBS-UP.

Yager dug in.

In came the pitch.

Yager blasted it.

The ball didn't go over the wall, but it found the left-center alley and caromed sideways off the fence. Hutt and Hall scored, ending the game.

Jalen could feel and hear the thunder of feet above him, shaking the stadium like an earthquake. Cat was screaming and looking into the camera at him. Daniel was hugging her neck and howling. The roar of the crowd swallowed them whole.

Jalen laughed and cried at the same time. Even though

he was alone, imprisoned in the Yankees manager's office, he knew everything was going to work out.

Relief washed over him. It was over, and he'd done it.

He didn't know if he could ever do what he'd done again, or if all the pressure had simply snuffed out his ability to predict pitches like a birthday candle.

But that didn't matter.

When he'd needed it, *really* needed it, Jalen had been a genius.

A baseball genius.

**What's next for baseball genius Jalen?
Find out in a sneak peek of**

> **Baseball Genius #2: *Double Play*.**

The policeman tightened his grip on Jalen's arm.

Still, Jalen grinned.

Up they went on a fancy elevator reserved for the Yankee Stadium suite holders. In the hallway, people with rolled-up shirtsleeves passed them, wearing curious faces. Jalen supposed the team employees stayed busy into the night if there was a game, and there had been a game, another victory for the Yankees.

Jalen's grin was born from something bigger than a win, even though the Yankees were his team. His was the grin of someone whose life was about to change. Someone who'd won the lottery or unexpectedly inherited a fortune from a long-lost relative. It was the smile of a kid who'd gotten the lead role in a play, or the MVP trophy at the team banquet. He wanted to share his joy, and he wished the policeman would ease up on his arm.

"Everyone looks happy with the game." Jalen smiled up at him, but the officer remained stone-faced. Of course, how could the policeman have known that Jalen's ability to predict the next pitch in an MLB game—or any game, for that matter—had helped the Yankees *win* the game?

They stopped outside a pair of wide, dark wooden doors. Jalen thought the officer was reaching for one of the heavy chrome handles, but instead he knocked. After a moment, he knocked again, and a stern voice ordered them in. Behind a mahogany desk as broad as a boat, the Yankees GM, Jeffrey Foxx, held a telephone to his ear. He pointed, not to the chairs, but to an empty space on the thick rug in front of the desk as he finished his call.

"You never were good at poker, Don." Foxx wore a scornful smile. "You're bluffing, and I'm going to double down. Good luck."

The GM hung up the phone with a scowl. He turned his attention to Jalen, staring with the pale eyes of a Siberian husky, vicious, hungry, and barely human. He had the tan skin and sun-bleached hair of a lifeguard, and Jalen was reminded of how tall the man was, even sitting at a desk.

The policeman finally let Jalen's arm loose. Again, Jalen

flashed his smile at the officer as he rubbed the blood back into his arm.

"Thanks, Jimmy," the GM said to the cop. "You can wait outside."

For a reason he couldn't explain, Jalen hated to see the policeman go.

"How about you take those sunglasses off so I can see you?" Foxx asked.

Jalen had forgotten about his glasses. He removed his hat and pushed them up onto his dark, curly hair. His eyes adjusted to the brightly lit office. In the window behind the desk, the stadium lights burned white and the empty field glowed, a rare bit of color in the concrete city.

"Those were so no one could see what you were up to, right?" The GM's frown deepened.

Jaden adjusted the glasses. "I guess."

"You guess." Without warning, the GM smacked his hand down on the desktop with the crack of an ax.

Jalen jumped.

Foxx leaned forward, planting his arms on the desk like he was preparing to pounce. His voice was a low, nasty growl. "Son, I have no idea why you're standing there smiling. You are in a *world* of trouble."